i

The Wide Turn Toward Home

Scott A. Winkler

Pocol Press

POCOL PRESS
Published in the United States of America
by Pocol Press
6023 Pocol Drive
Clifton, VA 20124
www.pocolpress.com

Publisher's Cataloguing-in-Publication
Winkler, Scott A.

The wide turn toward home / Scott A. Winkler. – 1st
ed. – Clifton, VA : Pocol Press, c2008.

p. ; cm.

ISBN: 978-1-929763-36-8

1. Baseball--Wisconsin--Fiction.
2. Baseball--Fiction 3. Self-realization--Fiction
4. Baseball stories 5. Short stories. I. Title.

PS3623.I663 W53 2008

813.6–dc22   0803

Cover photo of author taken by Martha Westphal.

ACKNOWLEDGEMENTS

For their love and encouragement, thank you to my parents, Albert and JoAnn Winkler, and my siblings, Christine Russell and Dave Winkler.

In more ways than I can name, you've helped this book come into being.

For a multitude of lessons learned and support on every level, thank you to St. Norbert College and the University of Wisconsin-Milwaukee, and especially to Ed Risden, George Clark, John Goulet, Sheila Roberts, and Kristie Hamilton. You were there that at critical times in my career as student, writer, teacher and scholar; your willingness to work with me and impart your wisdom have proven invaluable.

For being readers and inspirations, thank you to my colleagues and to my students past and present. Thanks especially to Pam Sylvester, Nancy Mannchen, Rod Ellison, Amy Linzmeyer, Elizabeth Costello, Jason Haedt, Meggie Greivell, Priscilla Hawthorne, Jessica Laurent, and Kassie Felix. May the lights that shine within you never grow dim.

For publishing early versions of stories appearing in this volume, thanks to *Elysian Fields Quarterly: The Baseball Review*, *Spitball: The Literary Baseball Magazine*, and *Sheepshead Review*. Special thanks to Tom Goldstein of *EFQ*. Your kindnesses have meant a great deal to me as I've gone through a difficult chapter in my life.

For being my friend, mentor, teacher, inspiration, and much, much, more, thank you to Tom Myers. From the moment I first walked into your classroom, my life changed. Cosmic tumblers truly clicked into place.

For being there as these stories came to life on our daily walks, thank you to Kramer. You're missed, but we'll one day meet again by the bridge.

And finally, for the sense of wonder that follows her wherever she goes, a sense of wonder that helps me to remember what really matters, thank you to my daughter Genevieve. Never be afraid to dream. Never let anyone tell you not to dream.

To Martha

With you, I'm forever safe at home.

TABLE OF CONTENTS

Burning Gorman Thomas

I remember slouching down in my desk and, behind the cover of a propped open grammar text, systematically scanning each of my Milwaukee Brewers baseball cards. My eyes traced the columns of statistics, and I speculated about how each player would fare as Mrs. Konen endlessly diagrammed prepositional phrases at the board. Her chalk scratched out lines and arrows in counterpoint to her nasal voice and the sound of someone's lawnmower drifting through the open window on an unusually warm October breeze. Not even Kim Stoltz, who sat in the desk ahead of me, her honey blonde hair falling down around her shoulders and smelling of flowers I couldn't name, could distract me from the task at hand. I made sure I tucked Gorman Thomas's card back into its proper place in the deck: fifth from the front—a practice I'd carried out all season, keeping the players arranged in the same order they batted, a practice that had created enough magic, I thought, to help the Brewers reach the World Series.

I had listened to games all that summer on the small Panasonic radio my parents had given me for Christmas. Some nights I sat at the kitchen table, my bare feet cooling on the old stone tile of the floor, and sipped Pepsi from sixteen-ounce glass bottles while Bob Uecker and Pat Hughes broadcast their play-by-play from Milwaukee or Baltimore or wherever the Brewers were playing. On these nights, I sketched out score sheets and recorded the storyline of the game in a shorthand of squares and squiggles, numbers and K's, circles and lines and arrows, creating a language no one else in my family could have understood. Other games I listened to from the porch jutting out from the second story of my family's farmhouse as a whippoorwill sang his three-syllable song from high in a black walnut tree and the warning light on the radio tower atop Suring Hill blinked red against the black night sky.

For day games, I took the radio to Grandma Kohls' trailer house across the lane from our house at the end of a dead-end road. She'd lived there since my parents bought the farm from her and my grandfather in 1972 and moved into the old farmhouse. Her house was one of my favorite places to visit. I'd put the volume on low as she stuffed me with Brach's spongy orange circus peanuts or peanut butter and honey sandwiches and told me stories about my mom's childhood and how my Aunt Margaret, the youngest of her three children, could have learned a few things from her older sister. The games typically didn't interest my grandma, so if she ran out of candy or sandwiches or stories, she'd sit in her old, brown-upholstered rocker and skim her Bible, quietly humming old Lutheran hymns.

When Mrs. Konen's voice and chalk stopped, I was afraid she'd called on me to identify the object of a preposition. But she hadn't. I followed her eyes to the door of the classroom. The last person in the world I expected to see was standing there—my dad. At first, I felt that heart-in-the-throat sensation—I thought that Shelly Woosnen had made good on her threat of telling the principal that I had snapped her bra strap during noon hour earlier in the week. Then I noticed my dad was still wearing his barn clothes, and I felt embarrassed. I hoped that he'd scraped the wedge of manure from his boots before coming into the school. He looked uncomfortable, shifting his weight from foot to foot, but our eyes met as he drew down the corners of his mouth and motioned for me to come with him. I got out of my desk and slipped a rubber band over the worn edges of my carefully-ordered cards before putting them into my pocket and stepping into the hallway.

Dad guided me away from the open doorway before speaking. "Your grandma—" He swallowed hard. "Your grandma is in the hospital." I grew dizzy for an instant. The fluorescent hallway lights seemed to flicker.

"She was shopping with your mom in Shawano when she collapsed. The doctor said it was a stroke." We walked to the parking lot and climbed into the old pickup truck. As we drove home, my dad said we'd do the evening chores and milking early, then go to the hospital. And he tried to explain, as best he could, what a stroke was. I imagined blood flowing along the lumps and curves of the brain, invading, pooling, coagulating. I pictured a brilliant young doctor deftly operating, staunching the flow, cleaning up the mess, repairing the damage.

I couldn't make sense of my grandma being in the hospital, though. I'd had a hard time keeping up with her when she took me flower picking with her in the hardwoods that summer. Just a few weeks earlier, she'd hiked two miles into the thickest part of the cedar swamp to pick the last of that year's wild blackberries. She could spend hours weeding her vegetable garden under an August sun. I felt confused and numb sitting there in the pickup truck—the same feeling I would have several days later when I tried to make sense of a strikeout while posthumous bombshells exploded around me.

2

All through chores and milking, my head swam. My dad and I spoke little. At one point, as I dipped a cow's teats with the orange-purple iodine solution, I imagined my grandma wearing a Brewers' road uniform and being carried off a baseball field on a stretcher. I was sitting in the first row of the upper deck, watching the scene from the narrow view beneath the top safety rail. Ballpark sounds and ballpark smells, jaunty pipe organ tunes and the scent of grilling hot dogs, swirled around me. The public address announcer, his amplified voice echoing off the concrete and steel and sounding like God, announced: "Elsie Kohls has now left the game. Kohls has left the game." In center field, Gorman Thomas stood with his glove hand on his hip, his meat hand stroking the thick mustache arching toward his jaw line.

When I awoke back in the barn, I was sitting on a bale of hay, my back to the calf pen across the aisle from the last half-dozen cows we'd been milking. Dad was holding my chin in one hand, gently shaking my shoulder with the other. Through the haze his voice grew louder each time he repeated my name, until it finally boomed over the roar of the motor that drove the vacuum pump of the pipeline milking system. "Albert! Are you okay?"

I told him I was and asked what had happened.

"When you stepped across the gutter, your foot caught in the chain of the barn cleaner and you fell." As I looked down at the wet, white smear over the length of my jeans—cow urine and barn lime—I realized that I must have passed out. I felt ridiculous. "Go in the house," he said. "Clean up. I'll finish up out here."

I didn't know what to think when we reached the hospital room. I recognized my grandmother lying in the bed. Tubes trailed out of her mouth and snaked out of her arm. A machine beeped regularly, and something that looked like a rubber-coated accordion flexed and compressed with an almost violent puff of air. The smells of antiseptic and plastic washed over me. My mom sat by the bed, stroking my grandma's arm, then looked up, her eyes red. She stood, but when she tried to speak, nothing came out of her mouth. She hugged me and cried.

Until that point, no specific emotion had really registered—it all seemed like an unreal scene from the television movies my parents watched when they thought I was doing my homework at the kitchen

3

table—but my mom's response triggered my reaction. My stomach flopped. Tears came in quick bursts, and a thick plug of mucous accumulated in my nose, forcing me to breathe through my mouth. My mom held me for a long time, until the tears ended and my mouth felt pasty, like something thick and sticky had dried on my tongue.

My parents told me to say something to my grandma—that she'd know I was there, that talking to her would help. They nudged me closer to the bed, then stepped back. When I looked at her, the queasy feeling came back and my breathing wasn't right. I put my hand on the rail of the hospital bed to steady myself. The chrome was cool beneath my palm. It seemed to settle me, and I began to breathe normally. I didn't know what to say, didn't see how she could know I was there, didn't know how anything I said would help. So I gave her the abbreviated play-by-play of the portion of Game One of the Series I'd heard on the truck radio on the way to the hospital, my dad's attempt to give me something else to think about. "Molitor led off with a single," I told her. At first, my tongue felt as if it belonged to someone else, but soon, the words came freely. My voice grew stronger. "Caldwell set the Cardinals down in order in their half of the first." I went beyond the play-by-play. I told my grandma how the Brewers would sweep the Cardinals in four games, how Gorman Thomas would be named MVP of the World Series, how she'd better get out of the hospital soon, before the whole thing was over, because I wanted to watch the final game with her at her trailer house where I would make peanut butter and honey sandwiches we'd eat from the china her mother had brought to America from Germany. I would explain what an RBI was, what ERA meant, how a pitcher could make a fastball rise and why a good curve turned a batter's knees to jelly. We'd watch as reporters interviewed players from the Brewers locker room and marvel at camera shots of 54,000 screaming fans swarming the field at County Stadium. Gorman Thomas, riding a Harley-Davidson, would circle the field on the warning track, and when he reached center field, he'd climb the fence and sprint up the bleachers to the gigantic beer mug where Bernie Brewer slid after every Brewers home run. He'd scale the mug, work his way up the slide to Bernie's chalet, and let out a war whoop as he waved an American flag in one hand, the American League pennant in the other. I didn't stop until I felt my dad peeling my hands from the bedrail and pulling me away. I was wired—my hands quivered, and I could feel the muscles in my neck tense.

My dad led me down the hall, past the nurse's station to a lounge.

There, he turned on the television to the broadcast of the game. The Brewers led 5-0. No lights were on in the room, and the glow of the television cast a bluish glow over the chairs and the magazines tossed on low tables. He stayed with me for a half-inning, saying nothing, just watching the game and glancing at me when he thought I wouldn't notice. "You okay?" he asked.

"Yeah," I said. "I'm better." I rubbed my hands down my thighs and sighed.

"I'm going back to the room, then—check on Mom and Grandma. I'll be back in a bit." I continued watching the game, and as the Brewers kept scoring, my spirits improved. Gorman Thomas went hitless, but that was okay—I just told myself he was saving his heroics for when the team really needed them.

My dad returned just before Mike Caldwell retired the final Cardinal hitter to complete his three-hit shutout. "There you go," he said. "Things are looking up." I couldn't help but smile as I touched the swell of the baseball cards in my pocket through the denim of my jeans. My dad suggested we return to my grandma's room. Without my parents' prompting, I walked to the bed and kissed her forehead. It smelled faintly of the perfume she put on too heavily each morning. I told her that I loved her and that I would see her tomorrow.

My mom stayed at the hospital as my dad took me home. We stopped at a McDonald's, where we each ate a Big Mac and an apple pie. We talked about the game. We talked about how Grandma would probably come home in a few days. We talked about Mrs. Konen and how my dad had had her as a teacher as well—how he and his friends had gotten in trouble for talking about her clothes. As we drove back toward home, a harvest moon hung bright in the sky. My stomach was full, my eyes grew heavy, and I went to sleep in the front seat of the truck.

Grandma Kohls died at 3:24 a.m. the next morning. The Brewers won Game One by a score of 10 to 0. She suffered a second stroke, and the doctors could do nothing. She never regained consciousness.

As relatives gathered over the next two days—my mom's sister Margaret from Ohio and her brother Otto from Florida along with his family—I kept to myself. I'd taken the portable television out of the kitchen and set it up on the dresser in my bedroom upstairs. I don't think my parents noticed; my dad was taking care of my mom, who wasn't handling the death very well—or the prospect of facing the younger sister to whom she hadn't spoken in years, the daughter my grandma had urged to be more like her older sister.

I watched the television broadcast of Game Two—a Brewers loss—from my bedroom. I sat on my bed with the wool flannel shirt my grandma had given me for my birthday a year earlier, mindlessly buttoning and unbuttoning it as the Cardinals rallied to take the lead in their half of the eighth. Gorman Thomas drove in a run in the game, but he struck out against Bruce Sutter, the Cardinals' star closer, with runners on in the ninth.

The day of my grandma's showing was an off day in the Series. The family gathered early at the funeral home. I remember feeling strange as I approached the casket—as though I was walking several feet above the ground. I cried. I hugged my parents. Relatives I rarely saw patted my head, clapped my shoulder, gave me looks that I now know were intended to convey sympathy, but at the time looked to me like figures from the slides of Munch paintings my art teacher had shown my class earlier in the semester. As my mom stood with her brother at the foot of the casket to receive visitors, I sat on one of the metal folding chairs near the back of the room. I watched my Aunt Margaret. She'd put on too much makeup—her eyelids were a heavy blue, her cheeks a garish red. She sank heavily into the velvet cushions of a sofa, and kept a flowered handkerchief in front of her mouth the entire time. I never saw her cry; if she had, her mascara would have traced liquid black tracks down her face, but I saw nothing of the sort. I really didn't know what to expect from her; she was rarely mentioned in our home, and her return for the funeral was the first time I'd actually seen her in person.

I studied the flowers arranged on either side of the casket—huge vases and arrangements whose scent made me feel sick. I studied the whorls in the grain of the casket's polished wood; it made me think of my shop teacher and the way he'd showed us how to use a finer and finer grit sandpaper as our napkin holders neared completion. I studied my grandma, my eyes focusing on her folded hands, looking for a gentle rise and fall that would tell me she was breathing, that this was all a mistake. When I did see such movement, though, I knew it was only my eyes, the dim lighting, and wishful thinking playing tricks.

Finally, I pulled the banded stack of Brewers baseball cards from my pocket. As always, they were arranged in the order they typically batted—Molitor, Yount, Cooper, and so on. Pitchers and substitutes followed the everyday players. I remember thinking, though, that these were special circumstances, that extra magic was needed. I pulled Gorman Thomas from the number five spot and placed him on top of the deck. He scowled back from the cardboard, his lips invisible beneath his mustache, his bat posed menacingly just back of his right shoulder. I smiled at him, slipped the rubber band back around the deck, and put the cards back into my pocket.

On the day of the funeral, immediate family sat together in the front pews as more distant relatives and other friends and acquaintances filtered into the pews behind us. Uncle Otto solemnly read the twenty-third Psalm. My mom read the story of the Ascension from the Book of Matthew. When she reached Jesus' final promise to his disciples, my mom broke down. As Pastor Kamke and my father guided her back to the pew, my aunt, sitting to my left, guffawed, a giant horse laugh that echoed off the stained glass windows even as she bit her bottom lip and quickly lowered her eyes. I could feel every eye in the sanctuary trained on our pew as my aunt studied the carpet, her cheeks growing even more flushed beneath her too-heavy rouge.

Pastor Kamke's sermon was brief. He spoke of my grandma's love of gardening, of the vegetables she'd given him and his family each summer since he'd come to serve our congregation. He spoke of my grandpa and how the two of them were now together. He touched on the significance of each of the readings. And he even mentioned me—how close my grandma and I had been and how fortunate it was for a grandparent to live so close to a grandchild.

Following the sermon, my cousin Mark, Uncle Otto's son, played his trumpet. I knew that he was working on a master's degree in performance at a school on the East Coast, but I'd never heard him play. His opening notes to "A Mighty Fortress is Our God" made the hairs on the back of my neck stand on end. He modulated keys as he played through successive verses and improvised a descant melody when the pipe organ joined him on the final verse. And when the pallbearers took their places on either side of the casket to guide it down the center aisle, Mark began to play one of my grandma's favorite spirituals; "Just a Closer Walk with Thee" began as a whisper, with no definite pattern, only the opening notes announcing the song. But as he continued, Mark built a version that moaned and wailed, that came to life. I saw my aunt roll her eyes and move her blood-red lips as she muttered something only she could hear, but I quickly forgot about her as the music swept me along. I imagined notes and colors floating in the air; I remembered Bible stories from Sunday School, of children coming to Jesus and crowds demanding miracles, of locusts and loaves and armies of trumpeting angels. We filed into the aisle behind the casket and followed it out of the sanctuary as the song's final notes echoed somewhere between the exposed rafters of the ceiling.

That night, the World Series resumed in Milwaukee. After chores and milking, my mom and her brother sat at the kitchen table, sorting through sympathy cards, writing out thank-you notes. Aunt Margaret sat apart from them in the old wooden rocking chair near the door to the living room. A couple of cards sat unopened on her lap, and she pulled back the curtains to look outside. I went to my room to watch the game.

In the sixth inning, with the Brewers trailing 3-0 and Gorman Thomas having struck out and popped out to the second baseman, I heard a knock at my door and a voice in the hallway. "May I come in?"

It was my cousin Mark. I normally saw him only once a year during his family's annual trip to the farm. When I was seven, we'd gone on a fishing trip with our fathers. As we sat in the boat, he kept asking me if I had worms. Not getting the joke, I'd dutifully reel in my line and check the glob of crawlers on my hook before dropping my line back over the side of the boat.

"How's the game?" he asked.

"Pretty much stinks right now," I said. "I liked your trumpet playing today."

"Thanks—just my little contribution." He told me how the bedroom he'd sleep in when his family visited each summer was next to my grandma's bedroom, how she'd get up at five-thirty every morning and whistle "Just a Closer Walk with Thee" before she'd put in her dentures. I laughed. We simply watched the game in silence for a while. I hadn't turned on any lights in my room, and the television cast a glow over us. The Cardinals scored two more runs in their half of the seventh.

In the bottom of the eighth, Mark asked if I really thought the Brewers could still win the game. "Of course," I said, and glanced at the banded stack of cards on my dresser, Gorman Thomas glaring from the top of the stack. "They've got magic this year." Bruce Sutter, the Cardinal's star closer, had already entered the game after their starter had taken a line drive to his leg and had to be carried off the field. Paul

Molitor grounded out to open the inning, but Robin Yount doubled over the third baseman's head. Cecil Cooper eased himself into the batter's box, his weight almost entirely on his rear leg in his wide-open stance. On a 2-1 count, Cooper turned on a rare Sutter mistake and roped it into the bullpen in right-center. "See?" I said to Mark.

"You might be right," he said. He got up from his seat. I heard him whisper a single word, "magic," as he left my room.

The next hitter, Ben Oglivie, flew out to center field. Gorman Thomas came to bat with two outs. He managed a single, a Texas leaguer on what even I had to admit was a lucky swing. But I remembered what I'd told Mark and crossed my fingers. Roy Howell struck out to end the inning. The Cardinals scored another run in the top of the ninth to win Game Three 6-2.

I returned to school the next day. My mind often wandered, and I remember sitting in fourth hour social studies wondering how Mr. Tietyen could ramble on about Minoan civilizations at a time like this. Noon hour that day was a plus, though, as Shelly Woosnen stood close enough to brush against me in the lunch line, smiling as she did. And in eighth hour, Kim Stoltz passed me a note at the beginning of class saying she was glad I was back. She dotted the "i" in her name with a heart and put her phone number at the bottom of the page. I distinctly remember hoping Mrs. Konen wouldn't call me to the board to diagram any sentences.

On the bus ride home that day, I thought about the warmth of Shelly's fuzzy sweater and wondered what it would be like to actually hold her close; I imagined the smell of Kim's honey blonde hair and pictured sitting with her in a dark corner of the gym at a school dance, just drinking in the delicate scent of flowers that seemed to follow her everywhere. And I thought about that night's Game Four, how the Brewers couldn't afford to fall behind three games to one.

As I left the bus, I heard voices from the driveway of my grandma's trailer house. Aunt Margaret was shoving a waffle iron into a U-Haul hitched behind her car, and Uncle Otto seemed to be pleading with her. "Look," he said, "if I get nothing, so be it. But what you're doing to them is wrong. Your sister has never done a thing to justify—"

"You're wrong there, dear brother," she said, poking my uncle in the chest with the impossibly long pink nail of her index finger. "She's done plenty—her and you. You both seem to have highly selective memory when it comes to family history." She slammed shut the open door of the trailer.

Uncle Otto's face grew red. He threw up his hands and walked away from her, shaking his head.

I entered our house and found my parents sitting at the kitchen table. My mom looked furious—her nostrils flared, and I could see a vein throbbing in her neck. "I can't believe she'd do that!" she said.

"Look," my dad said, "we'll just have to get along as best as we can. Maybe we can rent a few acres from Herman Kirsch or Bake Neuman—"

I let the screen door close behind me. "What's wrong?"

Mom snapped. "Why don't you ask your aunt—or your grandmother. Here—" my mom shoved a book across the table. "This is yours. You'd better hide it before your aunt packs it into the U-Haul with everything else." It was my grandma's Bible.

My dad stood up from the table. "Go up to your room and change clothes," he told me. "We'll start the chores."

I placed the Bible on my dresser, pulled on my barn jeans, and slipped into one of my dad's old shirts. I was confused—I knew something had happened that day, that something wasn't right. As I walked back through the kitchen, my mom stopped me. "Your grandmother was always good to you," she said, "and I suppose that's what you should try to remember. But mark my words, I will never forget what happened in that lawyer's office today—and Margaret can go to hell."

I'd never seen my mom like this. I didn't know how to respond, so I just stood there, awkwardly waiting to see what else she'd say. She got up from the table, went to the refrigerator, and pulled out leftover ham and scalloped potatoes from the meal the Ladies Auxiliary had served in the church basement following the burial. She set the temperature on the oven, the pilot light whooshing once as it began its task of heating, and looked at me. "When you're on your own, you'd better make sure you look out for yourself, because you sure can't count on anyone else to do the job." I wanted some sort of explanation, but I was afraid to ask. She spooned scalloped potatoes into a pot, put the ham into a blue-enameled Dutch oven, and said nothing more.

I wanted to say something to my mom, but was scared that it would be the wrong thing, that my words might make the situation worse, so I went to the barn and began my daily ritual. I tossed bales of hay from the mow, then carried them out to the feeder in the fenced-in yard where we kept our heifers; mixed powdered milk replacer with warm water and fed the calves; and limed the center aisle of the barn so the cows wouldn't slip when they lumbered into their stanchions for milking. And all the while, I tried to make sense of what I'd seen, what I'd heard.

After spreading the lime, I went outside and walked around to the rear of the barn where my dad stood watching haylage spit out the silo chute and climb toward the feed wagon on the elevator's moving flights. I asked him what had happened.

He told me that the will had been read earlier that day, that my grandma had left everything to my aunt with instructions for her to divide the property as she saw fit. He spit into the dust of the haylage that had settled at his feet. "We've been awfully good to your grandma, but since your aunt divorced that pig farmer, she hasn't had a bit of contact with anyone in the family."

"That doesn't make sense," I said. "Why would Grandma give her everything?"

"I wish I knew." He cranked the orange lever that lowered the silo unloader, then continued telling me about the day's events. "Your aunt didn't come back to the farm with the rest of us after things ended at the lawyers' office. An hour later, she pulled up with a U-Haul trailer and started emptying your grandma's house. A half-hour after that, the realtor came." He told me how an agent from Rupiper Realty had arrived, slipped a pair of rubber boots over his dress shoes, and started walking the forty where my grandma's trailer house sat, jotting notes as he went.

When my grandparents had sold my parents the farm, they'd set up the trailer house on a plot of land they'd kept for themselves—an insurance policy of sorts. As children of the Depression, my grandparents hedged their bets, reasoning that if things ever became bad enough for them, they could always sell the timber and charge my parents rent for the field they otherwise worked for free. The trailer itself sat on an acre of lawn with a garden to the north and apple, plum, and cherry trees scattered over the rest of the yard. Behind the trailer, a twenty-acre field stretched over gentle swells of loamy soil before ending in a stand of mixed hardwood and cedar. And now my aunt was going to sell it. "Probably to Genkes," my dad said, referring to our neighbors who'd just added another 150 cows to their herd. "With that many animals, they're hungry for the land."

As we milked that night, my aunt left for Ohio, the U-Haul trailer stuffed with everything she could fit from my grandmother's home. My uncle came to the barn and told us that seeing her lurch up the road was like watching the Clampetts during the closing credits of *The Beverly Hillbillies*. My mom walked with him to the sliding door at the far end of the barn. They stepped outside, and as my dad and I finished the milking, I could see them talking, kicking at gravel stones and shaking their heads as though they could think of nothing else to do.

I'd always thought my parents, and especially my mom, had been good to my grandma. They let her take milk from the bulk tank, and they gave her as much meat as she wanted whenever they butchered. Grandma didn't drive, so my mom took her everywhere she needed to go—to church each week, out for groceries every Friday, into Shawano or Green Bay when the occasion called for it, to Oconto Falls for her medical appointments. My mom mowed her lawn each week and tilled her garden each spring. They had canned vegetables together, put up preserves together, hilled and picked each other's potatoes together.

Looking back, I can almost understand my aunt's actions. She wasn't wealthy, but according to my mom, as the baby of the family, she had grown accustomed to getting what she wanted. She'd married a sweet-talking pig farmer and they'd moved to Ohio. He did more drinking than farming, though, and before long, he ran off with "Miss Ohio Pork Princess, 1971." Aunt Margaret didn't move back to Wisconsin and her family, though; she stayed in Ohio. And in all the years I'd taken my grandma her mail after school (always a good excuse to get a piece of hard candy), I'd never seen a letter or a card with an Ohio return address.

Game Four of the World Series was played that night. Again, I watched it in my room, and again, my cousin watched a couple of innings with me. I asked him if he knew anything about what had happened. He said that he did, and he told me a story, a bit of family history I'd never known, something his dad had told him after the reading of the will. Mark told me that my aunt had been pregnant when she married the pig farmer.

"What?" I said. "But she doesn't have any—"

"I know," Mark said. "Grandma insisted Aunt Margaret get married right away, and she did—but it was at the courthouse instead of the church. Grandma wasn't happy about it. Margaret was her baby though, so when she asked Grandma for the money she would have spent on her wedding and given her as a gift, Grandma was going to do it—until your mom and my dad convinced Grandma that probably wasn't such a good idea considering the circumstances."

My aunt's actions suddenly made sense—but so did my mom's and my uncle's, I thought. My aunt made the bed she slept in. "But what about the baby?" I asked.

"My dad doesn't know. Miscarriage? Abortion? Adoption? He couldn't say for certain. Just that she doesn't have any children now."

I knew Mark would be leaving in the morning. A part of me wanted to hide away in the back seat of his Datsun and go with him, to leave behind the mess growing around me. I hated seeing my mom so bitter, and I didn't want to think about whether what she and my uncle had done was right. I didn't want to think about my grandma's will, whether it was or wasn't fair. I remember thinking that I could ignore those things—that they'd eventually go away—if I could just leave home for a while. And I figured that once Mark had found me in his car, he would at least make sure I'd see the remaining games of the World Series—the one thing I could still pin my hopes on.

The Brewers had the magic in Game Four. Because Bruce Sutter had pitched over two innings the night before, Whitey Herzog, the Cardinal's manager, held him out of the game—good news for the Brewers. The Cardinals had taken a 5-1 lead going into the seventh, but the Brewers scored six times in their half of the frame and held on to win 7-5, tying the series at two games apiece. Gorman Thomas singled early in the game. He struck out during the seventh inning rally, but did rob Willie McGee of a certain double with a wall-crashing catch in the eighth inning.

My mom's mood improved little in the days that followed. She looked pale, and the skin on her face seemed to hang looser. She ate little, and she spent a considerable amount of time going over bills and that year's financial projections. When I would ask if she was okay, she would only say, "Cows can't feed themselves. Come next year, we need that land."

I saw little of my dad, other than during milking. He'd begun picking corn—a time-consuming job that found him sitting for hours at the wheel of the Case tractor, pulling the cornpicker as its mechanical teeth stripped each of the shriveled, brown cornstalks of its ripened ears.

13

He returned to the fields each night after milking.

My school days were a mix of everything other than studies: worrying about my mom, questioning my grandma, unsuccessfully trying to let my mind wander to the cute girls in my classes, and thinking about the World Series. The Brewers had put themselves in the driver's seat after Game 5, beating the Cards 6-4. Mike Caldwell had won his second game of the series, and Robin Yount had made history, becoming the first player ever to record two four-hit games in the same World Series. With a 3-2 lead in the Series, the Brewers only had to win once in St. Louis.

Game Six was a disaster. The Brewers lost 13-1. Gorman Thomas struck out three times and misplayed an easy fly ball in center. The Series would all come down to a Game Seven.

Figuring the Brewers would need extra luck, I made special preparations to view the final game. After milking, I took a quick shower and grabbed a Pepsi out of the refrigerator. I slipped a book of matches into my pocket, then went into the closet where my mom kept our holiday decorations and took several candles. In my bedroom, I placed my grandma's Bible on top of the small television and arranged the candles on my dresser on either side of the screen. When I lit them, their light was reflected in my mirror. The combination of the dancing, doubled flames and the light of the television screen made my walls seem to shimmer. When the Brewers were at the plate, I removed the baseball card of the batter from my rubber-banded stack and tucked it between the cover and first page of the Bible. When the Brewers were in the field, I put the card of that night's starting pitcher, Pete Vuckovich, in the same spot. I had also pulled all of my Cardinals cards from the collection I kept in a shoe box, and when one of them would come to the plate or take the mound, I'd draw a thick, black X over his picture with a chisel-tipped felt marker.

My baseball voodoo worked for the first five and one-half innings. The Brewers led 3-1, but in the bottom half of the sixth, the Cardinals scored three runs. They added another run in the eighth. With just three outs remaining, the Brewers trailed 5-3.

Predictably, Whitey Herzog brought in his star closer, Bruce Sutter. I looked at his card in the half-light of the dying candles and the television. A wide beard fringed his face. His eyes were ice blue, and his mouth was twisted in a smirk. On the screen, as he toed the rubber, he wore the same expression. I got off my bed and placed my grandma's

14

Bible in my underwear drawer and began connecting every swear word I knew with the name "Bruce Sutter". *Rotten asshole Bruce Sutter*, I thought. *Dirty bastard Bruce Sutter*. And I kept thinking such combinations as he struck out Robin Yount and Cecil Cooper. Ted Simmons, the Brewers catcher who'd played with the Cardinals for ten seasons, brought hope, though, as he lined a clean single to right field. The next hitter was Gorman Thomas.

"Yes!" I shouted at the screen. My hero, that season's American League home run champion, walked to the plate—two outs in the ninth inning of the seventh game of the World Series, and he could tie the game with a single swing. I remembered a newspaper article that had quoted Thomas: "People come to the yard to see me do one of three things—go deep, crash the fence, or strike out. I always give them one of the three." He'd already crashed the fence twice during the series, and he'd certainly struck out—his whiffs far exceeded his hit total for the Series, a paltry three.

I reasoned it was time for his third specialty. I brought my grandma's Bible back out of the drawer and whispered a brief apology for the dirty words. My hands shook. I felt sweat bead on my forehead. Thomas fouled Sutter's first pitch back into the screen for strike one, watched the second offering miss low and away, and took a called strike two.

The broadcast put up a split screen as each player readied himself. Thomas stepped out of the box and wiped his nose on the sleeve of his jersey, pulled at the crotch of his pants, and waggled his bat in the direction of the pitcher. Sutter stepped off the rubber and threw the ball to his catcher. The home plate umpire tossed him a new one. He rubbed it between his bare hands before sliding his glove back on and tucking the ball into its pocket. In the tight camera shot, his eyes were the same icy blue from the baseball card, and his mouth was twisted in the same smirk. The screen went back to the familiar center field camera shot. Thomas stepped back into the box. Sutter went into his stretch. I nervously bit at a hangnail.

As soon as Sutter released the pitch, I saw it would be out of the strike zone. Gorman Thomas didn't see the same pitch I did. He swung desperately as the pitch reached the plate at ankle level. Sutter had burned him. The Cardinals' catcher leaped into the air, the team rushed the field, Gorman Thomas dropped his bat, and I cried.

The tears lasted for a short time, maybe a half-minute. When

15

they ended, I felt empty. I turned off the television. Most of the candles had burned out, so I turned on the overhead light above my bed and gathered up the Brewers baseball cards in no particular order. When I picked up my grandma's Bible, I noticed a dark edge barely sticking out above the gold-edged pages and opened it to the marked page. The bookmark was a picture of my aunt, an old graduation picture. I began reading from the pages it marked. My grandma had bracketed a passage in the Book of Luke—a parable, the story of the prodigal son. *Nice story*, I remember thinking, *but that's not the way things really go*. When I'd finished the passage, I ripped the page out.   The thin paper made a hissing sound as I tore.

I remember that my head was throbbing. I picked up the stack of baseball cards from my dresser. I stepped into the hallway and heard the faint clicking sound of adding machine keys as my mother worked downstairs. I walked to the door leading to the porch that jutted from the second story of our farmhouse.

The mercury vapor yard light made the trees in the yard cast severe shadows that stretched out until they eventually blended with the night. A barn cat stalked something I couldn't see. I looked to the east and saw the outline of a Rupiper Realty sign stuck into my grandma's yard. Beyond that, the headlights of the tractor streaked into the night as my dad picked corn, a final harvest from the field someone else would work next year. I sat down, my back against the cool hardboard siding of the house, and stretched my legs out in front of me. With my thumb, I fanned the deck of baseball cards, then set them down. I held up the page I'd torn from my grandma's Bible and ripped it in half, then ripped the halves in half and tucked them under the stack of cards. I pulled the book of matches from my shirt pocket and breathed deeply. When I exhaled, my breath formed a faint cloud of vapor in the cool October air. I took the first card from the stack—one of the Brewers' set-up men, Jamie Easterly. I lit a match and held it to the corner of the card. The flame caught, and the card slowly burned as I held it up so that the fire wouldn't catch my skin. With the final corner of Jamie Easterly, I lit the next card in the deck, a process I continued until I reached the final card—Gorman Thomas. I let the second to last card burn down to a nub I had to blow out, then picked up the quartered page from the Gospel of Luke and wrapped the pieces of torn paper around the Gorman Thomas card. I lit one more match and held it to the paper and cardboard, then watched the flame steadily advance. When the paper and card had burned down to the final corner, when the last of the flame began to lick the skin of my thumb and index finger, I flung the bits of paper and cardboard toward the sky and spoke a single word—"magic." Orange sparks faded to black, and ashes drifted silently to the ground, too small for me to see when they finally landed on the grass below.

The Genuine Article

    The red dust of the back roads completely filled the creased leather of Isaiah's shoes. On this April morning in 1952, the old man was entering Oxford, Mississippi. He squinted at the sun rising over the cotton fields just outside the town. *Mmm-hmm*, he thought, *keep climbing. Chase those aches out of his joints.*

    Isaiah's pace was slow but certain. He had no need to rush, taking his time as he moved from one town to the next. The choice of night-time travel was deliberate—the sunshine may have been good for limbering up old pitchers, but it didn't make walking backroads any easier. More than one person, when they discovered his means of travel, told him he was crazy—"Ain't you scared, mister? Haven't you heard 'bout what some of those crackers like doin' to our kind?"—but he wasn't afraid. He reached into his pocket and pulled out a scarred silver watch, opened its lid, and checked the sweep of the hands. *Making good time*, he thought. *Be right on time.*

    When Mary opened the shade, the sunlight crawled over the sheets and woke Sam Simmons from a troubling dream—old faces he hadn't seen in some time had been speaking to him, but the words that left their lips were inaudible, and the more Sam asked them to speak up, the more desperately they spoke, their lips opening even wider, their eyes frantic. But at the warmth of the sun, Sam sat up, ran his long fingers over the stubble poking out from his deeply creased face, and slowly rose to his feet, unwinding his old man's frame—still taut as piano wire—to its full six feet seven inches. As he surveyed the glow around him, the memory of the dream slipped away somewhere among the winged dust particles dancing in the light and the sepia photographs hanging like icons on the cracked plasterboard. His lips curled into an easy, elastic grin.

    This was the day Sam had anticipated all winter, just as he did every year—ghosts stirred, the sun was brighter, the breeze lighter, the grass no longer the uncut hair of graves but a soft carpet for men at play, their passage marked by tracings in the red earth and preserved in columns of meticulous calculation. It was a day when people could marvel at these exploits and pass their stories to the next generation like heirlooms.

    It was Opening Day for the Oxford Black Giants, and Sam would take the mound against the Indianapolis Clowns. To anyone who'd followed the Negro Leagues, Slim Sam Simmons was the stuff of legend, but to the average fan of the game, he was virtually unknown. He didn't spin yarns like Satchel Paige or keep a mistress in every whistle stop. His nickname lacked pizzazz. Those who knew him best witnessed a quiet litany—Sam climbing the hill every fourth day, April through September, each of the last thirty-odd years. Sam did what he'd been born to do— pitch. And he did it without fanfare or ceremony, without hordes of reporters detailing his every move.

Sam had played nearly every avenue of organized baseball open to a Black player in his lifetime—in the great Negro National League with the likes of Buck Leonard and Ray Dandridge; on barnstorming teams, at times donning the absurd costumes which perpetuated stereotypes but gave him the opportunity to play ball—the ridiculous white face of the Ethiopian Clowns, or the bare torso and grass skirt of the Zulu Cannibal Giants; he'd even worn a long false beard and sidecurls and was billed as "the Jewish Moor" while playing with the integrated House of David traveling club. It was a hard life, but Sam could no more deny his love of the game than the gifts which were his birthright—a nimble arm and pinpoint control. The moment Sam stepped between the foul lines, uniforms, stereotypes—they didn't mean a thing. It was only the game that mattered.

On this Opening Day, Sam felt particularly spry as he shuffled off to the kitchen on his floppy galoshes feet. Only the pills were left to remind him of the November stay in the hospital. Yes, his blood pressure had been a bit high, and yes, his chest had been a bit tight, but the doctor hadn't found anything definitive, nothing he could point to and say, "That's all for you, Sam Simmons. Time had to come sooner or later. It's for the best." Instead, the doctor had told him to watch what he ate, take things easy should he feel something coming on, and to swallow the small white pill twice daily. The experience had scared both Sam and Mary, but secretly, Sam viewed it as a blessing in disguise. The hospital bills had put an end to Mary's hints that he ought to consider retirement— being a solid draw on the hometown club didn't make Sam rich, but it kept a monthly check drawn to the hospital.

Mary stood at the stove, stirring a blue enameled pot filled with ham hocks swimming in black-eyed peas, a mixture she'd keep over a low flame all day until the meat practically fell off the bone. She was a husky, good-natured woman and enjoyed razzing Sam, but she seldom

19

kept up the old nag act for more than a few minutes at a time. She looked out the window at the dirt road running past their home and watched a stranger slowly pass by. Sam walked into the kitchen and leaned over her shoulder. "Morning, sugar." He lightly kissed her cheek and patted her large bottom, letting his palm and long fingers come to rest long enough to give her flesh a gentle pinch.

Mary turned toward Sam and swatted at his hand with the wooden spoon. "What's gotten into you, you dirty old man? Sit yourself down. You oughta have that dirty old mind on other things."

Sam winked at her and took his seat. "Mmm-hmm. I'm just waiting on my breakfast. How's this dirty old man gonna toss strikes without his breakfast? Us old coots need all the strength we can get."

"You just keep them horses in the barn, mister," Mary said. She carried a plate and a cup to the small, oilcloth-covered table where Sam sat. It was the same breakfast he'd eaten—both home and away—the mornings of games he pitched all through his career. The only addition to today's menu was the pill Mary also set before him. Sam bowed his head for a moment, then broke the cake of coarse cornbread and lifted a piece to his mouth. He chewed slowly, then sipped from his glass of juice.

A rookie (of course) had once inquired about Sam's breakfast ritual—didn't it ever bore him? And it wasn't that tasty—not like sitting down to a plate full of bacon, eggs, and sausage with a cup of hot, black coffee steaming alongside the plate. Sam had told him you never mess with what works, that for him, this meal practically guaranteed success. It had been carefully calculated it to maximize every aspect of his performance. He kept it simple, like his pitching strategy—throw strikes and change speeds. The corn bread was heavy and stuck with a man for some time—fuel for the later innings. The downside, though, was that unless you had something to keep you regular, it clogged you up something fierce. Grape juice did the trick. All in all, it was an unbeatable combination. The rookie shook his head and looked at Sam as if expecting something more. "It is," was Sam's only response.

Sam turned to Mary. "Sugar, you sure we can't head back to the bedroom for a bit before I leave? It'll give you something pleasant to think about when I'm not on the mound, leave you a little smile that folks'll look at and think, 'now what's that Mary Simmons got on her pretty little mind now?'"

Mary raised her eyebrows. "It'll make me think of you, all right—probably give me the heartburn."

Sam chuckled. "Now you know better than to flatter me so." Sam popped the last of the bread in his mouth, took a long draw from his juice, and brushed the crumbs from his fingers. He placed the pill on his tongue, then washed it down with the last of the juice. "Sam Simmons is a new man—big things today, my sweet. Big things."

The contest was a home game and the Giants' home park, Jordan Field, lacked colored locker rooms, so Sam and the rest of the Giants suited up in their own homes. Sam dressed in the bedroom. He pulled on his white flannels with the black and orange piping, looped his glove over his belt, slung his cleats over his shoulder, and gave the brim of his cap a tug before stepping back into the kitchen. "Now what do you think, sugar—every inch the gentleman, hmmm? Once upon a time you wouldn't let me out of the place once you'd laid eyes on this striking figure of manhood."

Mary scanned him with narrow eyes. "You'll do for an old fart." Mary walked to him and pulled his wrinkled face down to her. They kissed briefly. "Now get yourself to the ballpark."

Sam gave Mary an exaggerated bow before pushing open the screen door and stepping into the street. The houses in their neighborhood were poorly built, but their irregularities were masked by the forgiving nature of tarpaper. Sam loped through the streets with an easy gait, and as always, young boys emerged, doors slamming as he passed by. At one house, a mother poked her head out the window, yelling after her son, "You leave him alone! That man has more important things to do than fool around with you little scamps!"

Sam stopped and called back to her, "Nah, it's okay. They don't mean no harm. Let 'em come."

The children clutched their own makeshift baseball gear and raced into the dirt road to see Sam in uniform, his home whites practically glowing in the sun. Their bare feet kicked up low clouds of red dust, and when enough boys had gathered, one always mustered the courage to ask, "Can we warm you up? Couldja toss us a few?"

Sam, as he always did, obliged. He took their baseball, usually a stone wrapped in yarn and electrical tape or a ball of tightly wound socks, and watched them form a diamond around him in the street. They took turns at bat, and before each of his slow, fat lobs, Sam cautioned them with a smile, shouting out, "Careful that this heater don't scorch you," or "This curve's gonna snap like a gator's jaws on a bullfrog—watch yourself." The boys swung a splintered bat held together with ten-penny nails. Whether they hit line drives or weak dribblers, Sam offered encouragement and advice—"Mmm-hmm, just like that. Keep that head down and swing level"—but it wasn't the authority of their swings that brought the wide smile to Sam's face. It was they way they showed their love of the game—it was simple and pure. Innocent. An uncomplicated love for the one thing they allowed themselves to believe in, especially now that they might get the shot Sam never had.

And after each boy had his cuts—"Three each," Sam said. "You boys wouldn't want me gassed before the game ever starts, would you?"—Sam resumed his easy gait toward the ballpark. On this day, as on most, a pick-up game started in his wake, and Sam knew it would undoubtedly continue until he walked home after his own game and the boys would pepper him with questions until their mothers called them in for dinner.

Sam warmed up in the bullpen along the right field line. The sun was unusually warm for April, but he was cooled by the sounds of the gospel choir from the Sweet Salvation Episcopalian Methodist Church, on hand to provide pre-game entertainment for the Opening Day crowd. Sam felt good—his arm was loose, and his assortment of junk balls shot in and out, dipping over the plate as if rolling off a table. And to his surprise, his fastball even made the catcher's mitt pop; he couldn't remember the last time it had done that.

The choir ran through a mix of hymns and baseball songs before wrapping up its portion of the pre-game with a rendition of "Amazing Grace" possessing more layers of harmony than an onion had skins. When the final line of the final verse rose from their lips—". . . and grace shall lead me home"—the word "home" hovered in the air like a fly ball as Sam cut loose with his final warm-up toss. The report of the horsehide exploding into the catcher's mitt echoed throughout the park. Sam's catcher, Rock Simonson, let out a howl. "Sheee-yite, Sam, what's Mary feedin' you for breakfast?"

Sam could only smile, shake his head, and think of the big things he'd promised his wife.

Mary took her usual seat in Section 1, Row 12, Seat 3. She knew the faces around her—Jordan Field regulars who'd warmed these seats since before Sam had come home to pitch for the Giants. There was

Marcus Hughes on her right, his score card rolled into a tube, and Lewis Hunter on her left, his straw hat tilted at its customary steep angle. In front of her, she recognized Terrence Anderson's orange-and-black suspenders and William Morrison, who'd already sweat through his shirt, a combination of nerves and nature.

One person, though, was new. Joseph Newsome wasn't perched on the edge of his seat to the left of Anderson and Morrison. Mary saw a slender man in his place, his head nearly bald. What little hair remained circled the fringes of the scalp with a snowy white that stood in stark contrast to the deep chocolate of the stranger's skin. As Mary settled into her seat, the newcomer turned. His eyes locked immediately on hers, and the corners of his mouth formed a gentle smile, exaggerating the endless wrinkles crossing his face. He wore old shoes covered in the red dust of the dirt roads. "Mary Simmons, it's a pleasure to be here with you today." His voice was warm and low, thick like molasses. "I've got myself a feeling about that husband of yours."

Mary drew a blank in trying to place the man speaking to her. The regulars looked equally puzzled. Mary spoke. "If you don't mind my asking, stranger, who are you?"

"Before that husband of yours ever threw his first pitch with the Crawfords, I told Mr. Gus Greenlee that a pitcher would be coming into the league who may not be the flashiest cat he'd ever lay eyes on, but that this pitcher would be flat-out one of the best ever—someone who'd leave his mark. That pitcher was your husband. I'd seen him barnstorming all those years before he hooked up with Pittsburgh. I knew what he was made of."

Marcus Hughes jumped in before Mary could respond. "Greenlee? The Crawfords? That was the greatest team money ever bought in the Negro Leagues! When Sam started pitching up in Pittsburgh, Cool Papa Bell played center, Josh Gibson was catching—"

"And Oscar Charleston at first and Satchel Paige in the same rotation with Sam. You know the game, don't you, Marcus."

Lewis Hunter adjusted his hat and eyed the stranger. "And you know Mary? And Marcus?" He licked his lips before continuing. "What's next? You gonna rattle off all our names? Give us the complete history of the Negro Leagues all the way back to the birth of Rube Foster?"

"You asking, Lewis? I got my sources."

William Morrison, his forehead shiny with perspiration, spoke.

23

"Who is you, stranger?"

The stranger's smile broadened. "My name is Isaiah," he answered. "Pleasure to make your acquaintance."

The tinny voice of the ballpark announcer crackled over Jordan Field's ancient P.A. system, calling out the names of the Giants as they trotted to their positions. Sam was the last player announced. He didn't bother fighting the goosebumps as he rose from the dugout and stood on the top step, the roar of the crowd washing over him. He tipped his cap toward Mary and the regulars. Marcus gave his scorecard a twist, and Lewis tipped his hat in return. Allen hooked his thumbs under his suspenders, satisfied by the acknowledgment, and William Morrison brought his handkerchief up to dab his brow. Mary and Isaiah smiled.

Sam began his deliberate stroll to the mound. Though he'd made that walk for three decades, though it seemed he'd toed the rubber of the mound in every ballpark in North America—from the hardscrabble clay of barnstorming through Manitoba to the manicured expanse of Yankee Stadium in the Negro Leagues' heyday—the thrill of standing on the mound to open the game never dulled, the feeling of one world letting go of boundaries and limits and another, ideal world opening up where time was measured in balls, strikes, and outs, not seconds, minutes, and hours. It was heady stuff for someone whose grandfather had been freed by Lincoln's emancipation, who'd been born to sharecroppers and remembered learning how to throw by flinging pebbles at birds in the branches of trees while his parents stooped over the rows of cotton beneath a relentless sun.

This Opening Day didn't start as well as Sam had hoped. The edge he'd had in the bullpen left him, and as a result of a pair of bad pitches and a fielding error, the Clowns took a 2-0 lead after the first inning. Mary shifted in her seat, unable to get comfortable, and wondered if she shouldn't have made a stronger case for Sam hanging it up during the off-season. She'd always thought it had been a heart attack, no matter what the doctors said. Maybe he wouldn't be the same. Isaiah turned to her and said, "Don't you worry, Miss Mary—that husband of yours is just taking his time. He'll find his groove yet, you mark my words."

Isaiah was right. In the second inning, Sam did find his groove, and over the next five innings, he didn't allow a hit or a baserunner. The opposition from Indianapolis looked just like their nickname—Clowns—

as they came up empty against Sam's masterful mix of darting sliders, tantalizing change-ups, sweeping curves, and the newly-resurrected fastball that had Simonson's glove hand throbbing. When the hitters did make contact, they either sent weak rollers to the infielders who scooped them up and fired frozen ropes to Thomas at first, or they sent high, arcing fly balls that dropped from the sky into the waiting gloves of the outfielders.

Mary began to feel more at ease. As Sam made quick work of the Clowns, she and the regulars in Section 1 grilled Isaiah—about his identity and how he could know so much, but Isaiah remained tight-lipped. He did, though, share stories about Sam that Mary thought only she knew. Between the sixth and seventh innings, Isaiah related an incident from Sam's one season pitching with an integrated semi-pro club in Saskatchewan. "This happened before you and him got hitched, see?" he said to Mary. "Charles Peterson, he was the regular center-fielder for the Canadians, and he was going to be married after a Sunday double-header against Saskatoon. So the club decides to throw him a bash befitting the occasion—roasting a pig out beyond the right field fence, buckets of Canadian pickled fish, food like you wouldn't believe. A local band is there to play some tunes, get the folks dancing, see? The club has everything you could think of—except any beverage other than water. No lemonade, no iced tea, no hard stuff—just these big old tubs of ice water.

"So Sam's pitching the second game and it's tied in the ninth, 3-3. The Canadians are coming up to bat in the bottom of the inning, but Sam starts to leave the ballpark. 'What're you doing?' says the manager. 'We don't score, I'm sending your ass out there in the tenth!'

"'Don't worry, skipper,' says Sam. 'We'll score; I've got some important business to tend to.' So the Canadians score. Peterson himself hits a homer—everyone teasing him that once he found out what married life was really like, he'd wish the game had gone into extra innings. So they all head out beyond right field for the festivities, and there stands Sam at the tubs of ice water, except they aren't filled with ice water anymore. Oh no. They're filled with wine, see? Everyone agreed it was the sweetest wine they'd ever tasted. To this day, no one has ever figured out how Sam pulled that switch. You ask him about it today, I bet he still wouldn't give away the secret. He'd only chuckle."

Mary didn't know what to say.

Sam's teammates had staked him to a one-run lead in the bottom of the sixth on a three-run homer by the Giants' dark-skinned Cuban third-baseman, Juan Bautiste. As Sam took the mound for his warm-ups in the top of the seventh, the crowd was buzzing and the choir was humming. They were witnessing a masterful performance—five innings of three up, three down, and if anything, Sam was growing stronger. The afternoon air was perfectly still as the ballpark announcer, his voice raspy from having shouted out introductions through a rolled program since the P.A. system sputtered and died in the fourth inning, introduced the Clowns' leadoff hitter, Bernardo Baro.

On the horizon, black clouds had been piling up since the bottom of the third. They now began rolling toward Jordan Field, but no one seemed to notice as Baro dug in at the plate. Sam made quick work of the Clowns' second baseman—a one-hop comebacker to Sam, who lobbed it to Thomas at first, but not before noticing something strange. Baro, as he ran toward the bag, wasn't Baro; Sam could have sworn it was the Kansas City Monarch's second baseman from the 1920s, Newt Allen, digging for first—something about the way he pumped his arms as he ran out the play.

Sam made quick work of the next two hitters as well, striking out the left fielder Griffiths and getting the right fielder Hassler to foul out to Simonson, but not before each of these players also raised the ghosts of players Sam hadn't seen in decades. Griffiths' stance in the box looked strangely like that of old Turkey Stearnes, and the twitching of Hassler's bat was identical to Mule Suttles'.

It happened again as the Clowns went down in order in the eighth. For a moment, each of the batters became a past teammate or rival in Sam's eyes—Buck Leonard, Ray Dandridge, Cool Papa Bell—only to become himself again as Sam wiped his brow with the back of his glove or looked back up after scuffing the pitching rubber. Two other people in the ballpark, however, had seen the momentary bewilderment flash across Sam's face as the players transformed—Mary, who wondered silently but said nothing, and the stranger Isaiah, who knew.

Mary scanned the clouds. From their color, she knew it would be raining—hard—before too long, one of those vicious hit-or-miss storms that streaked across Mississippi in the springtime. The first rumblings of thunder rolled over the field, and Mary thought she might have seen a brief flash of lightning in the distance.

Mary clutched the metal armrests of her seat, then leaned forward to watch her husband make ready for the Clowns' leadoff man in the ninth, a young shortstop named Henry Aaron.

Isaiah turned to the regulars around him and said, "Keep an eye on this Aaron. The kid's got it in spades. Today isn't his day, though."

After Sam chased the image of Jesse Williams from the young shortstop's face, he snapped a nasty 1-2 screwball. Aaron sent a weak one-hopper to Bautiste at third. "Can I believe what I'm seeing, you old man?" Thomas called from first after starting the ball around the horn. "That really you?"

"You'd better believe it is," Sam replied. He took Bautiste's return throw and tucked it into the pocket of his mitt. He felt the tingle of pin pricks dancing down his arm and shook them away before speaking again, this time to himself in a low voice. "The genuine article."

The Clowns' next batter, Jim Gilliam, stepped to the plate, a large man with a brooding expression. But when he twirled his bat in the box, Sam knew it wasn't Gilliam, but a man Sam had faced only once before the demons that eventually killed him sent him to the institution, convinced Kenesaw Mountain Landis was about to let Negro boys play in the big leagues.

Rube Foster stood at the plate, knocking the dirt from his spikes.

Sam motioned Simonson to the mound. "You seeing anything…strange about the hitters?" Sam asked.

"Other than the fact that you've got 'em scared out of their jocks, no, not really. Why, what you seeing, Sam? Everything on the level? Heat's not getting to you, is it?" Simonson noticed that the color had left Sam's face, leaving him ashen as he refused to take his eyes from Gilliam.

"No, no—I'm good. Just thought I'd check."

Gilliam—or Foster, or whoever the batter was—couldn't touch Sam's offerings—three pitches, three strikes, second out of the ninth.

Simonson called time and motioned the infielders to the mound before the last hitter stepped in. "Hang in there, Sam. You're almost home." He instructed the infielders on positioning for the final hitter, and warned them to be ready for the unexpected, perhaps a drag bunt or a Baltimore Chop.

Sam's teammates, though, appeared more uptight than Sam as

Simonson instructed them. Thomas punched his balled left fist into his mitt as Andrews and Josephs, the middle infielders crouched on their haunches and flicking pebbles away from the mound. Juan Bautiste, trying to lift Sam the only way he knew how, kept telling him, "Man, you are the one!"

Let's just not do anything stupid here, Sam thought. He felt the tightness in his chest squeezing, and he tried to breathe deeply, the rush of air in his lungs making him wince as his teammates returned to their positions.

The next batter due up was the Clowns' pitcher, their number nine hitter. Every person in the park thought the same thing—chalk one up for the history books. The Clowns, though, weren't about to write this one off; down by a run, they were only one swing away from tying the ballgame. They sent a pinch-hitter to the plate.

The announcer shouted out the name of the pinch hitter—"Now batting for the pitcher, #40, Lenny Pearson." And as the name was called out, the rain began—not a light drizzle that would increase in intensity, but an immediate downpour, sheets of rain making the outfielders barely discernible to Sam from the mound. The umpires, though—perhaps sensing the moment at hand—made no move to clear the players from the field. The fate of this batter would be determined now.

Sam's jaw nearly hit the ground when he looked toward home for his catcher's signal; that wasn't Pearson digging into the box, but another dead man looking very much alive. Sam rubbed his eyes with the back of his hand to make certain the rain wasn't making him see things. His chest squeezed. It was him, all right.

Sam motioned Simonson back to the mound. "What am I supposed to make of *that*?" Sam rubbed the ball between his bare hands and nodded in the direction of the hitter without taking his eyes off him.

"What're you talking about, Slim? You seeing ghosts or something?"

"Well look at him."

"Pearson? He couldn't buy a hit off you all last season, and with your stuff today—hey, let's get going before we have to ride this out back in the dugout."

"Pearson?" Sam asked, sliding his glove back on.

"Yes, Pearson—you sure you're okay, man? Nerves is understandable, and this rain isn't doing anyone any favors, but hang in there—you're one away from the finest game these folks have seen you throw in years."

And as Simonson trotted back to the plate, Sam ran the toe of his shoe over the rubber and eyed the batter. He was improbably barrel-chested with legs far too spindly for such a torso. His ankles were almost delicate, his small feet pigeon-toed, and as he dug in with left foot, his back turned toward the mound, Sam saw the number "40" fade from the hitter's uniform to be replaced with a black number "3".

There he was, the hitter Sam had never faced in a game that counted. He'd only faced him in exhibitions, when he'd come to the plate chomping on a cigar, more interested in mugging for the fans than anything else. Now, he tugged at the brim of his tiny cap and raising a massive bat to his shoulder. He looked back at Sam from a round, moon-shaped face with a wide, flat nose. Sam was being stared down by Babe Ruth.

Mary saw it, too—it was as if the deluge had washed away gauze from her eyes, giving her true vision. Ignoring the rain, she grabbed Isaiah's shoulder and was unable to let go. "What's going on here?"

Isaiah turned to her with the same smile he'd worn all afternoon. "You see it, don't you?" He turned back to the field. "Just watch," Isaiah, said. "Just watch."

No matter what Simonson said, Sam knew it was Babe Ruth standing in the box. He didn't doubt that the Bambino deserved his reputation as a great player—even chomping on that cigar years ago, he'd hit three monstrous foul balls off Sam before going down on strikes. Sam, though, knew of a hitter who was even better, a former teammate who'd died five years earlier of a brain tumor, a half-empty bottle of whiskey the only witness to his passing. Sam closed his eyes for a moment and pictured him, the way he'd stood at the plate, feet wide, the thick muscles in his forearms twitching beneath his dark skin as though possessed of a life all their own, the compact swing that made balls jump off the bat like they did for no other player. There was only one Josh Gibson, and when Sam opened his eyes once again to look toward home through the rain, he saw that Ruth no longer stood at the plate. *That's better*, Sam thought, *it's only fitting—good to see you Josh*. Sam rocked into his motion and painted the outside corner of the plate with a change-up.

29

Strike one.

When they'd been teammates, Sam and Josh had liked to debate whether Sam would've been able to get him out. "I'm the big, black Babe Ruth, you know," Josh liked to remind him, referring to the description the sportswriters more often than not associated with him. "Except Babe Ruth was never so handsome—I'm too pretty to get out."

Sam would laugh it off and assure Josh that though he might be able to make frequent contact with the fairer sex, he'd come up empty against Sam—but he'd never tell him just how he'd do it. Sam's second pitch was a slider, low and away. Gibson swung, but came up empty. *Always did like to go fishing, didn't you, Josh.*

Gibson called time and stepped back from the plate. He twisted the handle of his massive bat in his hands, knocked the mud from his cleats, and looked to the mound. Sam's eyes held Josh's stare, and for a moment, each of them smiled. One pitch, Sam thought, the tightness in his chest now radiating. The hitter nodded to Sam, but before he stepped back in, as if sensing the moment, he raised his right hand and pointed to right field, mocking the Bambino's famous called shot in the '32 Series. *Not on your life*, Sam thought, knowing his old friend was trying to goad him into putting a fastball in his wheelhouse. Nobody handled high heat better than Josh—Sam had seen him hit one ball over 700 feet against Satchel—so Sam reminded himself of what he always told himself to do against the sluggers: *Think softer*.

The rain actually increased in intensity as Sam reared into his wind-up, reaching back with an arm that no longer felt his own, every nerve ending pulsing with intense sparks that turned to fire as he planted his right foot, leaned forward, and let his arm follow.

The instant of the occurrence seemed to play out at 1/100th of normal speed, allowing—for better or worse--everyone in Jordan Field to see Slim Sam Simmons send a humpbacked eephus pitch toward the plate; see Josh swing at, and miss, the ball twirling tantalizingly in the air; see the umpire raise his fist to signal strike three; see Sam stumble in his follow-through and fall to the mound, clutching his chest.

Everyone in the stadium rose at once, though the multiplicity of events prevented a uniform response. Some whooped to acknowledge the third strike, a celebration of a brilliant performance. Still others cried in disbelief at the sight of the fallen pitcher lying on the mound.

Isaiah remained in his seat, head bowed, chin resting on the thumbs of his folded hands. Mary went down the steps, clambered over the low wall, and went to her husband. Players from both teams circled the mound. Sam lay in the dirt, unmoving. Mary knelt over him. Thomas knelt also, his ear just over Sam's nose, listening for the sound of breathing.

Isaiah raised his head, stood, wiped the rain away from his brow and looked out over the field. He reached into his pocket, pulled out his scarred silver watch, and checked the sweep of the hands. Several players rushed to the mound with a stretcher as Isaiah walked to the exit and left the stadium, his pace certain, the kind of pace that carries a man where he needs to be.

Lezcano

I bought Lezcano shortly after my nasty, brutish, and short marriage ended. My ex hadn't allowed me to own a dog while we lived under the same roof, so when she moved in with the man from the realty where she worked—the one I'd always referred to as Sasquatch whenever I saw him at holiday parties—I began looking for a dog. When I came home from a day of teaching high school creative writers who couldn't write complete sentences much less master verisimilitude, I wanted to be welcomed by someone actually happy to see me. A dog seemed the logical choice. I'd grown up on a farm. My family had always owned Black Labs, so I began inquiring about classified ads boasting "AKC registered Lab puppies, hips guaranteed, parents on-site." None of the puppies, though, gave me the *that's the one* feeling, so on a whim, I checked on a litter of Doberman Pinschers.

As soon as I knelt down to look over the squirming mound of feet and ears, one of the puppies pulled himself off the pile, waddled over to me on feet four sizes too big, and sat down. He was bigger than the rest of his littermates, and unlike his black and rust brothers and sisters, he was a deep gray-blue and rust. He cocked his head and looked at me, then raised an over-sized paw and waved to me. When I scratched him, he squirmed appreciatively and his cigar butt tail wagged at what seemed a hundred miles an hour. He tugged at my shoelace, growled playfully, and looked up at me for my response.

The matter was settled.

I wrote a check to the breeder, received the necessary papers, and drove home with a twelve-week-old Doberman Pinscher curled up tight against my thigh on the front seat. The moment we entered the house, the puppy scrambled up the stairs, turned around, and flashed a vaguely familiar puppy smile that implored me to follow him. So I did, watching him skid over the hardwood floors: through the kitchen, the dining room, and into the living room, where he stopped in the middle of the area rug—a hideous contemporary thing my sweet ex had left behind when she crawled into Sasquatch's cave. Puppy squatted and made a neat pile of number two atop intersecting squares and circles my ex had called "harmonic geometry." The puppy flashed me that same vaguely familiar smile, and in a moment of recognition, I placed it—it was the exact grin worn by former Milwaukee Brewers right fielder Sixto Lezcano on his

32

1979 Topps baseball card, a favorite from the collection I'd kept as a boy, the collection my mother had unwittingly thrown out after I left for college.

"Here, Lezcano," I said, and he came to me without hesitation. When I scratched him, he seemed to have too much skin—it bunched and wrinkled on the lithe body that would quickly grow into it. He licked my fingers, and I chuckled as I looked at his pile of number two. "Good aim, Lezcano," I said.

I knew we'd get along just fine.

Fortunately for me, Lezcano loved baseball.

After taking the rug out to the curb, I took out the toys I'd bought in anticipation of bringing home a puppy—a plastic porcupine that made a high-pitched squeak when squeezed, a blue nylon ring covered by soft nubs, a hollowed out natural cow bone, a tug-of-war rope. Lezcano inspected each of the items, but none of them held his interest. Before long, he made his way through the open closet door. He sniffed the floor, licked a pair of leather hiking boots, and made his way to my baseball glove. He stopped just short of the mitt, tipped his head to one side, and hunkered down, his front paws extended straight out in front of him. He stretched one oversized paw toward the glove, reached into its pocket, and quickly pulled his paw out. The baseball nestled deep in the pocket appeared like a scoop of vanilla ice cream atop a cone. Lezcano pounced, and the ball squirted out onto the floor.

For the next hour, I watched him play with the baseball—rolling it, leaping at it, playfully growling at it, until he finally lay down with it between his front paws and alternately licked it with his soft pink tongue and gnawed at the tight red laces. That night he began a ritual he would continue for the next fourteen years—sleeping next to me on the bed, his chin propped atop a baseball.

Lezcano's second night in my home, I discovered that he also liked watching America's pastime on TV. It was late October, 1988, and that year's World Series between the Dodgers and the A's was set to begin. After returning from school, I played hard with Lezcano to burn off his energy and to tire him out so that he would, I reasoned, sleep during the game. As the broadcast was about to begin, I took my favorite spot on the couch, popped the top on a cold beverage, and put my feet up on the coffee table (another thing my sweet ex wouldn't have approved of). Lezcano sat on the couch next to me with what was now his baseball

33

resting on the indentation between the cushions. From the moment Bob Costas began his play-by-play, Lezcano was glued to the screen. Occasionally, he'd prop his head on his baseball or let his tongue loll on its white horsehide, but his eyes never left the screen unless I'd ask him what he thought about a play or a managerial decision. In those instances, he'd look at me, his head tilted slightly, and release a breath that puffed out his cheeks as the air escaped.

That night, we were both treated to one of the great moments in World Series history. In the bottom of the ninth, the Dodgers' Kirk Gibson came to the plate as a pinch-hitter against the most dominant closer in baseball that season, Dennis Eckersley. Gibson had suffered a severe leg injury in the National League Championship Series. Most observers had expected him to miss the World Series completely, yet there he was, barely able to walk to the plate, sent to bat on a hunch by Tommy Lasorda.

"So, Lezcano," I said, "what do you make of this?"

He puffed his cheeks, looked at the screen, then looked back at me and whined softly.

"I agree," I said. "Gibson's as gutsy a player as you'll find, but look at him—he might as well be standing on one leg. Eck is gonna eat him alive."

Lezcano opened his mouth as wide as he could and stretched his tongue well beyond the tip of his jaw. Then in a single motion, he pulled in his tongue, snapped his mouth closed, and shook his head from side to side. I could hear the loose skin of his jowls flapping.

Eckersley came at Gibson with his herky-jerky sidearm delivery and quickly rang up two strikes. I scratched Lezcano behind his ears. "It doesn't look good, bud," I said. Lezcano panted. I leaned forward, reaching for the remote, ready to turn off the television as soon as Eckersley struck out Gibson—I'd promised my first hour class I would return their attempts at villanelles, and several still waited for my comments.

Those poems never got graded that night—my ability to concentrate was gone after what happened next. When Eckersley sent his two-strike offering toward the plate, Gibson lunged at the ball. His bat made contact with a low, outside sinker, and the ball kept rising as it streaked toward right field and landed in the bleachers of Dodger Stadium, a two-run homer that gave the Dodgers Game One of the Series. It was the kind of moment boys playing ball on long summer days imagined in their perfect visions of the future—nothing at all like their wives taking up with gangly realtors.   I dropped the remote when the ball landed several rows back in the right field bleachers. "Oh my God," I said. Lezcano sat on the couch and stretched his nose toward the ceiling. Deep within his puppy chest, a howl built. It started surprisingly low and rich—not a sound that I expected from a twelve-week old puppy, even if he was a Doberman Pinscher—and then rose steadily in pitch and intensity, climbing at least two octaves. The howl filled the room completely, bouncing off the walls and rattling the picture frames on top of the entertainment center, and to this day, I swear I saw my empty beer bottle move several inches to the right across the surface of the coffee table.

Lezcano became my best friend. He understood my moods, accepted my faults, and was always happy to see me come through the door. He was the star of his obedience school class—he could heel, square, down, come, and stay like nobody's business. He helped me get into shape with our daily walks. And aside from that first night, he never did a number in the house—he seemed to instinctively know that if he went to the patio door and gave three short barks, I'd come to let him out.

And, of course, from April to October, we always had baseball. We both loved the Brewers. During the regular season, we'd watch the cold weather games on television, but during the balmy nights of summer, we'd go out to the patio, turn the radio on low, and listen to Bob Uecker and Jim Powell. I'd lean back in a lounge chair, and Lezcano would lay on his favorite blanket, close enough for me to reach down and scratch him. The Brewers never made the post-season in those years, but that never stopped us from watching the World Series. We witnessed the infamous earthquake game in '89, Jack Morris's gutty ten-inning shutout against the Braves in Game Seven of the '91 Series, the Marlin's improbable defeat of the Indians in '95, and the Yankees' dominance of everyone starting in '96, when they captured four of five World Series.

The Yankees. The damn Yankees.

I hated them, and so did Lezcano. They were good—too good— and I wanted to see someone, finally, knock them off their throne. I'm sure Lezcano did, too—on mornings after Yankees won a World Series game, we were both in foul moods. Lezcano wouldn't explore the yard when I let him out before leaving for work—just take care of business and come back to the patio door to be let in. And my students knew that it would be the middle of fourth hour before I was capable of a civil response to anyone.

During those years, Lezcano grew old. The pace of our walks slacked, and the enthusiasm with which he chewed baseballs went down a notch or two. In '97, I started giving him painkillers for arthritis. By '99, he needed hip replacement—I know, you're thinking "hip replacement for a dog? Isn't that a bit extreme?" Yeah, it is—and expensive, too—but I had it done anyway. It took away the pain and even made it a bit easier for him to accept the Yankees winning it all every year, but it couldn't hold back time completely.

By September of '01, Lezcano's once blue and rust muzzle had gone completely white, and arthritis had moved into his front hips. Two days after the terrorists destroyed the World Trade Center, the vet told me that Lezcano had cancer. What a pisser of a week. The vet advised against surgery—"He's too old, and there's no way I could be sure of getting all of it. At some point," he said, "you're going to have to make a decision about euthanizing him." I hated the word—just the sound of it coming out of the vet's mouth made me cringe, made me picture needles and eyes going dim and a worn baseball that would never be coated in dog saliva again. And I hated it all the more because I knew the vet was right.

Things got tough for Lezcano by the third week of October. We could no longer go for even a short walk. He was having a hard time keeping down food, and he had his first accident ever in the house (I don't count that first night as an accident; to this day, I'm sure he knew what he was doing). But when the World Series began and Arizona took the first two games from the Yankees, he seemed to take a turn for the better—he was even waiting for me at the door with his leash when I came home from school one afternoon. The Series proved to be a seesaw affair as the Yankees took the next three games; two of the victories came in dramatic fashion, coming in their last at-bat off Diamondbacks reliever Byun-Yung Kim. By the time Game Six rolled around, Lezcano was again having a hard time eating. The Diamondbacks won the game in a convincing manner, forcing the decisive Game Seven. Lezcano managed to hold down half a can of Eukanuba.

I laid out Lezcano's favorite blanket and helped him up onto the couch for the final game of the Series. By the start of the seventh inning, Lezcano's breathing had grown shallow. By the top of the eighth, he'd begun to shiver, and I pulled his blanket up around him. As the ninth inning began, Arizona held a slim lead; as the interval between each of Lezcano's shallow breaths grew longer, I gently lifted his head to rest on my lap and slid my hand beneath the blanket to reach the spot behind his front shoulder where he liked to be scratched.

Just before the Yankees tied the game to send it to the bottom of the ninth, I thought I'd lost Lezcano—it must have been at least thirty seconds since I'd last felt the barely perceptible rise and fall of his ribcage beneath the blanket—but when the tying run crossed the plate, I felt him inhale deeply. I couldn't hear it, but through the denim of my jeans, I could feel a low growl rumbling in his throat.

It wasn't over yet.

Tony Womack singled for Arizona in the bottom of the inning— poetic justice, as his error in the top of the ninth had led to the Yankees scoring the tying run. As Womack rounded first and scampered back to the bag, the camera shot showed him looking up and pointing toward the sky. The announcer reminded viewers that Womack's father had died earlier that season. Beneath the blanket, heat began to radiate from Lezcano—I could feel the palm of my hand sweating, then feel that perspiration actually evaporate from my skin as he grew hotter and hotter. The same heat spread out from where his head rested on my thigh, but as intense as the heat became, it somehow didn't burn me.

The Diamondbacks managed to move Womack over to third base, and as Luis Gonzalez stepped into the batter's box, a weird calm filled the room. With the exception of the space between the couch and the television, the air became opaque, a milky white that I know, had I reached out to touch it, would have felt like warm gelatin. I could only make out the faint outlines of my bookcases, of the end tables and floor lamps, of the stairs to the basement. I could smell fresh-cut grass and the loamy scent of rich soil. The television's speakers quit working, and Lezcano stood up on the couch, slowly turned around three times, and sat tight against me, still radiating the heat that somehow didn't burn.

We both watched in silence as Gonzalez, choking up on his bat at least two inches in an effort to handle the fastballs of Mariano Rivera, looped a single into left field, watched in silence as Womack crossed the plate with the winning run, watched in silence as his teammates mobbed him at home plate, piling on top of each other, a squirming mound of sheer joy. Lezcano and I looked at each other. He grinned the same grin that had prompted me to give him his name and then licked my face.

37

Deep within his chest, I felt the howl build. He stretched his nose toward the ceiling and opened his mouth. The howl started low and rich, then rose steadily, filling the room completely. A shower of sparks bloomed from the television, and a split second later, a crack the shape of a lightning bolt etched itself into the screen. Lezcano's baseball rose from the couch and hovered in mid-air in front of me, spinning like a curveball. A wave of heat washed over me as my head filled with a brilliant, silent white light and I lost consciousness.

I awoke to darkness. The digital clock on my VCR blinked *12:00* over and over, and my mouth felt pasty, my tongue thick and reluctant to move. I reached to turn on the lamp. No response. When my eyes grew accustomed to the darkness, I could make out the outline of Lezcano on the couch. As I stumbled toward the basement stairs to grab a flashlight, I felt as if I was walking several inches above the floor. I had to grip the handrail as I descended the stairs, opened the door, and reached around the corner for the flashlight.

When I turned back toward the living room, it took several seconds for me to fully grasp the scene. Every light bulb in the room had shattered, and the tiny slivers of glass sparkled in the beam of the flashlight. The lightning bolt was still etched in the television screen, and similar cracks had appeared on the glass of picture frames around the room. A Galileo thermometer had split open, spilling water and its floating glass bulbs, also broken, across the top shelf of a bookcase. The baseball that had spun in the air before me was lodged in the wall above the couch. And Lezcano, or more properly the form of Lezcano, lay quietly on the couch. He was drained of all color; no deep red brown, no rust markings—just a flat, gray surface that otherwise revealed every contour of his body. I reached across the flashlight beam to touch him. The tip of my index finger had scarcely brushed his surface when he imploded, forming a Doberman-shaped mound of ash. Wisps of smoke curled into the air, dancing weird patterns in the flashlight's beam.

Lezcano had spontaneously combusted.

When I awoke the next morning, my head throbbed as if someone were striking my bald spot every three seconds, and even the faint halo of sunlight seeping around the blinds made my eyes feel like they were burning. I groaned and turned over, throwing my arm toward the spot where Lezcano typically laid. When I found only cold, rumpled comforter, I forced my eyes open and looked to the dresser where a ceramic piggy bank in the shape of a baseball resting on a catcher's mitt sat next to the too-red digits on the face of my alarm clock.

When Lezcano's form had collapsed in a low pile of ashes on the couch, I vacuumed them up with a hand-vac, emptied the bank of coins, taped over the slot, and poured the ashes into the hollow sphere. I continued cleaning the living room. My mind seemed to have floated away from my body as I worked; though I was aware of what I was doing as I picked up slivers of glass, I felt like I was sitting in the upper deck of a stadium, watching myself. I didn't know whether to laugh or cry, so I did both—alternating jags of no more than a minute each—and then felt compelled to dust my entire house from top to bottom. I went through three packages of dry wipes, cleaning off literally everything—the tops of doorframes, the moldings along the stairs, the tops of light fixtures, the cover of the toilet tank, the programmable thermostat.

After dusting, I brought Lezcano's ashes to the kitchen and placed the bank on the table. I went to the refrigerator, opened a package of hot dogs, nestled two of them into buns, and wrapped them in paper towel. A minute in the microwave heated the hot dogs and steamed the buns—the closest I could come to ballpark cuisine without actually being there. I squirted lines of ketchup and mustard along each of the hot dogs and spooned tangy green relish onto each of them—Lezcano liked relish. I took two orange sodas from the refrigerator, then sat down at the table across from the bank holding the ashes and pushed a hot dog and one of the sodas toward the bank. I ate my hot dog slowly, chewing thoroughly, letting the flavors of hot dog and condiments spread over my tongue. The soda's carbonation sent a pleasant burn from the back of my mouth down my throat. After I finished my stadium fare, I cradled the bank in my hands, went to my bedroom, placed the bank on the dresser, and climbed into bed fully clothed.

My jeans were twisted uncomfortably around my left thigh as I lay in bed that morning, my head pounding. I showered but didn't bother shaving, then crawled into my most comfortable sweats and pulled every W.P. Kinsella book I owned off the shelves and took them to the bedroom. I'd lost someone I loved, it was a Sunday morning, and I needed religion.

After I opened the shades, propped my pillows against the headboard and sat down on the bed, I began thumbing through the worn pages of the books. Slowly, carefully, searchingly, I read stories of baseball and time travel, of ghosts and redemption, of lithe Caribbean shortstops making impossible plays thanks to voodoo priests, of college second basemen who choke under pressure and find homes in rural Iowa playing for teams that exists in name only, of a former player who deposits the ashes of a deceased teammate in the concrete pilings of the Metrodome as it is being built in Minneapolis. I don't know exactly how long I read—I'd switched on the lamp mounted to the headboard at some point, and I must have left the bed to remove Lezcano's ashes from the dresser, because I found the sealed baseball bank on the bed, tucked against my leg at the spot where he liked to wedge himself—but I do know that I drifted off long enough to dream.

In my dream I was carrying the bank with Lezcano's ashes through a mausoleum filled with a fine, floating mist. My rubber-soled tennis shoes squeaked on the polished marble floor tiles, and I remember shivering as I caught a glimpse of myself reflected in the markers that lined the walls floor to ceiling. When I stopped to look more carefully at the markers, I immediately noticed that the inscribed names belonged to deceased baseball players. I mouthed their names as my eyes wandered over their plaques—Eddie Matthews, Roy Campanella, Josh Gibson, Donnie Moore, Dan Quisenberry, Jackie Robinson, Ted Williams. The cool porcelain of the bank grew pleasantly warm in my hand, and I smiled. I walked toward the exit of the mausoleum. I was thirsty, but finding no bubbler, I instead drank from my cupped hand holy water from the basin mounted on the wall, and I walked out into a perfect summer afternoon. A woman worked in a flowerbed, and she smiled at me when I paused to watch her. Her hair was straight and mousy brown. It nearly reached her shoulders, and she wore a pinstriped late-1970's Brewers jersey. On one hand, she wore a flowered gardening glove, the kind with rows of tiny rubberized dots on the palms and fingers, intended to help with grasping gardening tools. The pace of her work slowed, and each of her movements was deliberate. She spread a fine, gray fertilizer over the soil, then raked it with a three-pronged tool—scratching, then looking at me, her eyebrows raised, then scratching again. This went on for several minutes. When beads of sweat appeared on her forehead, she reached into her gardening bag and removed an old-fashioned hand fan, opened the clasp, spread it open completely, and fanned herself. After she'd cooled herself, she stepped out of the flowerbed, stood in front of me, looked at me with her green eyes flecked with gold, and gently kissed my forehead in the heartbeat before I awoke.

Convincing the head groundskeeper at Miller Park that I was legitimate wasn't that difficult, even over the phone—I dropped the name of a small liberal arts college for which, I lied, I maintained the baseball field. I'd researched lawn care at a local garden center and had picked the brain of a member of the grounds crew at an area golf course, so I began talking about the nitrogen content of fertilizer and the necessity of aeration, about the pros and cons of mowing every other day versus every third day, about proper soil conditioning and optimal watering rates. Before I knew it, he'd invited me to visit Miller Park to observe him and his crew as they gave the field a final once-over before shutting down their operation for the winter.

I placed Lezcano's ashes in a Ziploc bag, took a day off from work, and went to Milwaukee. I watched as the groundskeeper and his crew mowed and aerated, spread pelletized gypsum and dragged the infield dirt. Most of the crew had left the field when the groundskeeper let me try out his favorite rake on the earth around home plate— "GardenPro X-3300," he said. "Get one of these babies, it'll be the only rake you ever need." So while he puttered with a shovel along the warning track in the outfield, I reached into my jacket and removed the Ziploc bag containing Lezcano's ashes. They'd grown warm, and because the November air was crisp, they felt good in my hands, their weight, their heat. I shook my head and chuckled, trying to imagine what Lezcano would do if he could see me at that moment. I slowly ran my thumb across the plastic, then opened the bag and gently emptied the ashes across the earth. I carefully raked them into the soil, just to one side of where the catcher crouched to wait for the pitch. "Play ball, friend," I whispered.

I'd been in college when the Brewers had last played in the World Series, a seven-game loss to the St. Louis Cardinals in 1982, and the years since then had done the club no favors—no more post-season appearances and only a handful of seasons in which their record had topped .500. They'd gone more than a decade without a winning record before reaching the Series that found me sitting in the right field bleachers, waiting for them to begin the decisive seventh game against the Yankees. Baseball scribes had pointed to a number of factors that led to the team's turnaround—the maturation of the team's young but talented pitching staff, the hitters' ability to lay off bad pitches and cut down on strike outs, the managerial change that had apparently breathed new life into a stagnant organization.

I chalked up the change to something else—the presence of Lezcano. I didn't regard it as coincidence that in the season after I'd raked his ashes into the dirt around the plate, the Brewers had enjoyed the most successful year in the team's history. He truly had, as I saw it, created magic for the club. The pitchers found the corners of the plate, and the hitters, many of whom had been on the team that just two years earlier had set the major league record for most strikeouts, put good wood on the ball and, in the proverbial words of Wee Willie Keeler, "hit it where they ain't."

On a hunch, I had Jim "Smokey" Burgess—a colleague, fellow baseball fan, and video technology buff in the English department at my school—put together a videotape break-down of Jenkins, the Brewers' left fielder. Jim superimposed, frame by frame, dozens of Jenkins' at-bats from the World Series season over those from the ugly campaign he'd endured the previous season. His stance hadn't changed at all, nor had the trajectory of his swing. What I did seem to notice, however, was that Jenkins' bat, usually in the twentieth or twenty-first frame of the at-bat, seemed to increase in length. Low, outside pitches that he'd flailed at in the past were now sent screaming down the line, just fair, for extra-base hits.

When Jim looked at the tape, he said, "It seems he's getting better extension on his swing—he's not opening up his shoulders quite so much, so he can stay on that outside pitch."

"Yup," I said. I wasn't about to admit what I noticed. Jim didn't need to know that Lezcano's ashes altered the laws of physics around home plate at Miller Park—just let him (and the sportswriters and the talking heads on ESPN) think what they wanted. No one was worse for it.

Three and a half hours before the game, traffic had already slowed to a crawl all the way back from the Miller Parkway off-ramp to I-94, and a somber October sky pressed against the earth. I drummed my thumbs on the steering wheel to Dr. John's version of "Take Me Out to the Ballgame." The mist falling in gauzy sheets beaded on the hood of my car. Below the off-ramp, I could see thousands of vehicles already arranged in neat rows, the parking lot lights glinting off their roofs and the slick asphalt. *Thank God for retractable domes*, I thought. I placed my hand on top of my thigh, over the front pocket of my jeans, and felt the swell of the folded twenty-dollar bills—$500 altogether, enough, I hoped, to score a ticket at a scalper's price to Game Seven of the World Series. For a moment, the steering wheel felt like a garden rake in my hands, and I looked at the snapshot of Lezcano that smiled back from the dashboard.

When I finally reached the lot and was directed to a narrow parking stall, I slipped into my poncho and pulled up the hood before leaving my car. It was warm outside—October days that gray and damp weren't supposed to feel balmy, but this one did. The mist was soft against my cheek as I walked down the rows of cars, past tailgaters flipping bratwurst and hot dogs on their grills, popping the tops on cans of beer with a quick pssst, turning up the volume of whatever music set the mood for them. I didn't have to wait long to find a scalper. He wore a ragged blue flannel shirt and walked with hunched shoulders. His hair was matted and looked like it hadn't been washed for several days. I didn't bother haggling, just handed over his asking price and checked the ticket—right field bleachers. Not where I normally liked to sit, but it would do.

Near the area of the lot called "Gantner's Garden" in honor of the Brewers' longtime second baseman, a bearded man motioned for me to join his tailgate party. His group had extended a blue plastic tarp from the open back of a rusty VW bus. I ducked beneath their makeshift shelter. The bearded man smiled at me. "Build the vibe, man—eat a brat for the home team!" he said before taking a healthy pull from his can of Lite. "Hey, Sharon," the bearded man said, "the dude's starving—load one up for him." I watched as a woman wearing a pinstriped late-1970's Brewers home uniform glided toward the food arranged in the back of the bus. I could only see her from behind as she worked slowly, almost deliberately, grabbing a squeeze bottle of mustard, spooning onions from a Tupperware container, tucking shreds of sauerkraut between the brat and bun. When she finally turned around, she held out the brat to me in her left hand. As I took it from her, I noticed that she was wearing a flowered gardening glove, the palm and fingers covered by rows of tiny rubberized dots. *It can't be*, I thought. I made eye contact with her and saw that her eyes were green with tiny flecks of gold. Her hair was straight, a mousy brown, and nearly reached her shoulders. Her mouth turned up at the corners, and she wrinkled her nose just before she winked at me.

The pitching match-up for Game Seven was a classic—the Brewers' ace Ben Sheets matching the Yankees' veteran fireballer Roger Clemens fastball for fastball, strike for strike. Going into the bottom of the ninth, the Brewers trailed 2-1, all the game's scoring the result of solo home runs in the early innings. The tension in the stadium was palpable, and by the time the Brewers came to bat in the bottom of the inning, the crowd noise mushroomed against the panels of the retractable roof and rolled back down over the standing room-only crowd. The man to my left, an elderly gentleman who had hobbled to his seat leaning heavily on a cane, had broken his cane over the metal railing in front of him when the Yankees had tied the score in the fourth—and was now standing under his own power, shaking his clenched fist toward the roof. The woman to my right had begun the game with a rosary clutched tightly in her right hand, counting beads and whispering Hail Mary's whenever Sheets struck out a Yankee hitter. By the bottom of the ninth, though, she'd tucked the rosary into her pocket and was standing, yelling in full voice with flecks of white spittle flying from her lips.

I seemed to be the only person who was calm when the Brewers' lead-off hitter, Ricky Weeks, stepped to the plate. The Yankees had brought in their closer, Mariano Rivera, to finish the game for Clemens, who'd lost some velocity in the eighth inning when the Brewers had nearly pushed across a run to tie the game. When Hall singled to right, the elderly man began stomping his foot, and veins stood out from the temple and neck of rosary woman. The next hitter, J.J. Hardy, showed bunt—not a bad move, I thought, to put Weeks in scoring position with only one out. Hardy took Rivera's first offering for ball one. Showing bunt had pulled in the Yankees at the corners, and though Hardy squared to bunt on each of the next two pitches, he took both of them, one for a ball, one for a strike. On the 2-1 pitch with the Yankees still pulled in at the corners, Hardy began to square again before pulling back and slapping a Rivera fastball past Mientkiewicz for a single. Weeks, who possessed good wheels and had been running with the pitch, went to third. Runners at the corners, nobody out—things were looking good.

Prince Fielder was the next Brewers hitter, and he looked to end the game with a single swing of the bat. Though that swing had clubbed fifty-five homers that season, it couldn't quite catch up with Rivera's high heat. The one positive during Fielder's at-bat was that Hardy stole second base. Jorge Posada, the Yankees' catcher, hadn't bothered to make a throw when Hardy broke from first, likely anticipating that the

Brewers may have set up a delayed steal that would have sent Weeks streaking toward home the moment he released the ball.

Bill Hall was intentionally walked to set up a double play, and the number five hitter, Estrada, went down on a called third strike. When Jenkins stepped to the plate, I could literally feel the stands vibrate. As I watched him dig into the batter's box, though, the crowd noise seemed to come to me as if through a heavy wool blanket, and with the exception of my sight line to the plate, the rest of the ballpark took on the same opaque appearance that had filled my living room that night in 2001. I held out my hand, touching the air. It quivered like warm gelatin. I thought of Lezcano.

On a 2-2 pitch, Jenkins slapped a Rivera slider (on the outer half of the plate, I would later notice on replays) into center field, a clean single. Weeks scored, and Hardy aimed to do likewise, ignoring the third base coach's desperate motions to stop. It wasn't a wise decision. Johnny Damon had charged the ball in center and came up throwing. The ball would clearly beat Hardy to the plate. The crowd's collective groan sounded as though it were gurgling through a substance not quite liquid, not quite air.

The shock came, however, as Posada was about to take Damon's throw. Behind the catcher, a blue-gray Doberman Pinscher literally sprang from of the dirt around home plate. Even from my seat in the right field bleachers, I knew it was Lezcano who hurtled through the air, the mercury vapor stadium lights glinting off his glossy coat. His body was fully extended, and his muscles seemed cut in bas-relief as he flew toward Posada. In an instant, Lezcano sank his teeth into Posada's right butt cheek, and the incoming baseball glanced off the catcher's mitt. Hardy slid across the plate with the winning run, and the umpire reacted instinctively, spreading his arms wide with his palms facing the ground—safe!

Lezcano, apparently seeing the misplayed throw, released his grip on Posada, skirted the catcher, and scooped up the ball in his jaws. He dashed over the pitcher's mound. Derek Jeter tried to tackle him, but Lezcano juked him, leaving Mr. *GQ* with an armful of infield dirt, and streaked toward the outfield, toward right field, toward me.

The elderly man to my left said, "I'll be damned," and rosary woman passed out. When Lezcano reached the warning track, he leaped, and defying the laws of physics, flew over the right field fence. The arc of his jump carried him directly over my head. Looking up, I saw him open his jaws and release the ball just before a silent white light washed over the bleachers, blinding me. When I regained my sight, I found the ball Lezcano had dropped cupped in my hands. I looked around, but couldn't see Lezcano anywhere. On the JumboTron in center field, though, images of the game's final play ran in slow motion—Hardy churning around third base; Posada, as a good catcher should, blocking the plate, waiting for the throw; Hardy going into his slide just as Posada took the throw and bent to slap on the tag. At this point, though, the scene on the JumboTron differed from what I'd witnessed moments earlier. Instead of seeing Lezcano materialize from the dirt to break up the play, I saw Hardy collide with the catcher, saw the ball squirt loose, saw Hardy scrambling to touch home. The screen froze momentarily on the scene before cutting to images of fans celebrating in the stands. A close-up of a woman with mousy brown hair and wearing a late 1970's Brewers home jersey stared directly back at me, her green eyes, flecked with gold, dancing. She punched the air with a gloved hand and smiled. I looked down at the ball I clutched in my hands—it was warm and covered with saliva, and with my thumb, I could feel the slightest indentations. Teeth marks. I looked back to the JumboTron, where the woman's lips blew a silent kiss that I could feel burning into my forehead with an impossible heat that spread over my entire body, washing me with love.

Come January

Even through her thick polar fleece, Monica felt the cold aluminum bleachers. She crossed her arms low across her stomach, cupped her elbows, and let the chill run its course. She'd grown to hate these September games in the low minors—a smattering of fans, the floodlights even dimmer than usual, the hot dogs even more shriveled, the innings dragging by at something slower than a snail's pace. And Rick—poised on the top step of the dugout like a cat ready to pounce should the manager glance in his direction and, with a nearly imperceptible jerk of the thumb, send him to the on-deck circle.

They'd known it was a long shot. Even the high picks faced dubious odds, but when Rick had been drafted in the fifty-second round by the Angels, neither of them questioned what he should do. They'd been married just three weeks after graduating from UW-Oshkosh, and the call from the Angels had come just after they returned from their honeymoon-on-a-budget—a long weekend at the Holiday Inn in Milwaukee, a trip to the zoo (Monica loved the aviary, Rick the baboons), an afternoon at the Domes, and, of course, the three-game home stand at Miller Park.

At the games, Monica watched Rick analyze everything happening on the field; she could almost see the wheels turning in his brain as he studied pitchers, and she couldn't help but feel his forearms twitch beneath the palm of her hand as he timed the pitcher's delivery to the plate. Between innings, when he smiled at her, his grin just left of center, and ran his thick fingers through her hair, she allowed the pleasant shiver run through her and whispered the single word they used as a substitute for "I love you" in public situations where such a profession would have been unseemly: "Bunt."

The torn knee ligaments halfway through Rick's third season had come close to bringing it to a halt. They'd originally agreed that if he hadn't made the Show by the end of his fourth season, he'd give up on the dream, they'd look back on it with a smile and no regrets, and get on with life as normal people did. Monica couldn't bring herself to tell Rick, but she found herself hoping that the injury would bring about an even earlier end to Rick's chase, perhaps let them live out of something other than suitcases and duffle bags six months a year. Monica's best friend from high school had just had a baby, and Janice, her roommate from Oshkosh had just finished her master's degree at Madison. Monica had started preparing applications to graduate school and began looking more and more often at the parenting magazines she kept at the bottom of her tote bag. She started clipping classified ads for Rick—phys. ed jobs in school districts near the universities to which she'd send her applications. Maybe you'll be able to coach there, too, she'd told him. But Rick looked at the clippings as motivation to speed along his rehab, and he thanked Monica for knowing just what it took to motivate him, to remind him of their dream.

Monica hated winter ball. The Dominican Republic had, at first, sounded better than another winter of her and Rick staying in the renovated bedroom in her parents' basement, the interminable hours Rick spent in front of a floor-to-ceiling mirror studying his swing, the endless nights spent breaking down his play on video. At least there'd be no subbing for bratty middle school students. But their room in the D.R. had paper-thin walls, and when the couple on the other side fought, they sounded like badgers growling in angry Spanish. And then there were the cockroaches. And the water that left red rings in the toilet and sink and tub and tasted like iron.

And the miscarriage.

"This is it," Rick had told her as he broke Spring Training with a Single A club in the New York-Penn League. "If it doesn't happen this season, it's over." Monica had watched as younger players received the bulk of playing time. She watched as Rick maintained his routine—always the first to the park, always the last to leave, sneaking extra cuts in the batting cage, fielding extra grounders during infield, running extra sprints before each game in the soft grass of right field, exhorting his younger teammates to step lively, pick it up, put the pedal to the proverbial metal as Monica warmed the aluminum through the crisp evenings of April and May, baked under the summertime sun, and shivered through the final games of September.

And Rick had started talking about playing winter ball again. Venezuela, or maybe Puerto Rico this time. Maybe the change of scenery would do them well, Rick had said. Maybe it would be good to put the D.R. behind them.

Monica reached into her tote bag as Rick's team took the field for the ninth inning—past the well-thumbed magazines, past a sheaf of job openings she'd tried to share with him before he'd left for Florida that February, and she removed the envelope with the Iowa City postmark. She hadn't told Rick about the acceptance letter. Instead, she called the department and secured permission to delay admission until the spring semester. She looked at the shriveled hot dog she'd set down alongside her, half-eaten in a stale bun, and almost gagged. Come January, she knew exactly where she needed to be.

And Now, a Word from the Beav

I've always liked *Leave it to Beaver*. Maybe it's just because I want down time when I get home from practice—some mental comfort food, meatloaf and mashed potatoes for the brain. Or maybe I just like to procrastinate when homework piles up. What would you rather spend time with: a trig textbook and differential equations (due at the beginning of the period tomorrow, or it's a zero in the gradebook, mister), or an idyllic bunch like the Cleavers?

Mostly it's because Beav and his family are so...*together*. They get it, even if it's only because they're a TV family steered by a bunch of McCarthy Era writers who didn't think viewers could stomach a dose of reality. June catches the Beav snatching a cookie or Wally gets mixed up in one of Eddie Haskell's crazy schemes, and it's a matter of "Just wait until your father comes home." Then Ward comes back from work, natty in his dark suit and skinny tie, and dispenses whatever fatherly wisdom is necessary to set things straight before everyone sits down for pot roast at a table draped in starched linens.

But what if the Cleavers weren't as together as they seem? What if we could hit a magic button on the remote and catch new episodes instead of the re-runs? Would they enjoy the same sitcom life? Or would Wally getting nailed for toking up with Eddie in the bathroom, would June mix a pharmacological stew to cope with her feelings of inadequacy, would Ward get home late from the office because he's getting a little something with his secretary? Maybe Beav would have ADHD and sell ritalin on the playground.

Maybe I'm stretching things a bit. I make the Twenty-First Century Cleavers sound more like the kind of family on a prime-time drama that gets bounced after a month. Worse, I'm being sacrilegious. The Cleavers are classic. They've got staying power—unlike my family. Too bad. I could use a double dose of Ward—I wish I could go to him, slicked up in his Fifties Brilcreme look, have him tussle my hair, give me wink, and flash that "it's going to be all right" grin. That's not what's going to happen when I break it to the old guy.

My mom says I don't have a choice.

I tried to reason with her, to tell her what a shitty time this is to break the news to him, but I suppose that would be true of almost any time, right? Does a father ever want to hear that? "C'mon, Mom," I said, "just awhile longer. He'll be all done. The season'll be over—he'll have said his good-byes and the nostalgia trip will have run its course. He'll have settled into a routine. He'll be better equipped to handle it."

But does she listen? "Wrong-o, Justin," she says. "That's not the way this family works. Not anymore. If you don't tell him, I do. No secrets. We deal with it. Period." In our family, though, "dealing with it" doesn't necessarily mean handling the matter constructively. Just ask my sister Stephanie how she felt after "talking" to the old guy when he missed her playing in the state volleyball finals because he was in Colorado taping a hunting special for ESPN. Or ask my mom about the time she confronted him about a certain red-headed baseball annie in Chicago.

But those are other stories for another time. The way my mom looked at the floor when she said "deal with it" freaked me out. She seemed to be counting the loops in the carpeting, her eyebrows sloping and the skin bunching in the middle of her forehead. Mom's a beautiful woman—looks about fifteen years younger than she really is thanks to Dr. Dale and the wonders of strategically placed collagen—but when she confronted me, she looked old. Old and tired—though that was an improvement over the "what the hell" look that twisted her face when she told me that she'd seen me with Alex.

I hadn't realized she was there. In a house like ours, you can lose yourself and anyone else in it. I thought Mom was out, working on a benefit cookbook with other players' wives. I hadn't heard her come home, didn't know she was in the kitchen overlooking the pool, didn't realize she'd seen me there with Alex, sitting on the steps in the shallow end, didn't realize she'd seen us kiss. When she confronted me later, my stomach dropped to my ankles and my palms began to sweat. It wasn't the first time Alex and I had kissed, but it was the first time I'd ever faced having to talk about it with my parents.

And my dad. God. I pictured that cheesy coming out show on MTV, where the camera follows you around, waiting for you to say, "Hey, Mom (or Dad), I'm...gay," and then the parent bursts into tears and the person who came out starts pounding on the wall, and when he speaks to the camera again he's blurry-eyed. You can hardly hear his voice and he's wiping snot from his nose with the back of his hand.

And wouldn't you know it—when Mom confronted me, I also thought of the Cleavers. Go figure. I pictured one of those "years later" specials where the Beav has come back from college at Christmas break, and sitting there over turkey, he keeps stammering, trying to get something out about a guy he met in a physics lab or at a frat party. Maybe Wally punches him in the shoulder, calls him a dope, and tells him to speak up. June, her motherly instincts blazing to life, senses something wrong and goes to the kitchen to make hot cocoa. And Ward. Gray at the temples, a few more wrinkles around the eyes that add to his look of perpetual wisdom, he knows just what to do to make everything better for the Beav.

The fact of the matter is this—telling my dad is going to be a pisser. For both of us. The old stoic won't show it, at least not on the surface. That's not part of his makeup. The legendary Joseph Steele, a blue-collar legend and certain first-ballot hall-of-famer. But then again, it's not like he's around enough for me really to have ever seen how he handles disappointment. I only see him during the home stands during the season, and even then, he gets home late and, because he's the great "Joey Ballgame," he leaves early to be the first player at the ballpark.

In big picture terms, it's probably just as well he's not around much—it might be better for everyone involved, give him some time to think, to acclimate himself to the "new" son sleeping in the bedroom down the hallway. Maybe he'll use this final season to decide what to do with me, how to act around the son who, like dear old dad back in the day, has all the tools and skills that make scouts drool. I'm projected to go in the first round next June. The only questions are how high and the size of the signing bonus.

By all appearances, I'm the reincarnation of the old man—the same wide shoulders, thick muscles, and slim waist, the same glowing tan and the wavy blond hair that helped score Joey Ballgame a contract modeling Jockey shorts early in his career. Like him, I play third base, hit to all fields, and have what the scouts call "intangibles." Like him, I've got my head on straight when it comes to work habits. Like him, I took the most beautiful girl in school to Prom—but in his case, that girl became my mother; in mine, it was all about keeping up appearances.

Mom has been so anal about "communication" ever since the old guy's affair became public. Once I tell him, the tension in the house won't be explosive. But it will be persistent—like the low-level rumble you feel when you're sitting by the window in a restaurant and some creep rolls past in a low rider, bass line rattling the glass, as if a trunk loaded with speakers compensates for something he knows he lacks. You know the type of moron I'm talking about.

I'm not saying my dad's a moron. I just have a hard time believing that a person so smart about one part of his life is such a dumbass about everything else. In purely baseball terms, my dad's a regular Einstein. I read the magazine articles about him. The article in *The Sporting News* after he'd announced he'd retire at the end of this season called him "the thinking man's ballplayer, a cerebral, intense throwback who will be sorely missed by his team, the fans, the very game to which he's given his everything the last seventeen seasons."

And whatever faults he has, I love my dad and am proud of his accomplishments. I've accepted the absentee father bit. It comes with the territory. And I may be seventeen, but I know that having a dad who pulls down eight figures per has its perks. When I watch him at the ballpark, he actually looks happy, has an aliveness in his eyes that's a departure from the vacancy there at home. He looks so in control, as if he can will the course of events as the game unfolds. At times, he almost looks like Ward Cleaver in double knit polyester pinstripes instead of a tailored wool sport coat.

Maybe my mom's right. Maybe I should just hit him with it right out, no bones about it, lay all the cards on the table. I'll be eighteen in a month, and if the signing bonus isn't big enough when I'm drafted, I'll head to FSU on a scholarship to hone my skills and wait for next June. And with this being his last season, he'll be spending more time at home come fall—a lot more time. No Spring Training. No calling my mom from a hotel somewhere on the East Coast. He'll actually be able to see me play ball if he wants to.

I'm scared. But then, maybe my dad will be scared, too. I know some sportswriter is going to call him half-way through next season to see how retirement is treating the great Joseph Steele. He'll ask my dad about his golf game, about how he thinks his replacement at third base is doing, about how, if he were still playing, he would've responded in some crucial situation in the late innings of a tight game. And the questions will eventually come around to how he spends time now that he's got it to burn, whether he's taken up any hobbies—woodworking? Fishing? And the family? How does it feel to be around them so much? Wife ready throw him out yet (snicker, snicker)? And the kids?

My dad will have the safe, canned answers to trot out for such soft-serve questions—"Golf game's improving…I wouldn't have tried to pull the ball, that's for sure—gotta hit behind the runner…They're great, Jim. I missed so much of their growing up that it's great just being around them."

But I can't believe those words will match his thoughts, match what he'd like to say but can't given his image as one of America's last great sports heroes—*I caught my wife thumbing through 'lawyers' in the yellow pages...that punk couldn't hold my jock...and my son? Seed of my loins? Faggot. A flaming homo. No place in the Show for that.*

The first time I kissed another guy, it just happened. Camping trip after sophomore year. It's not some elaborate drama—it just *happened* even though it scared the hell out of me. I've handled it in my own way since then. End of story. Sometimes, something comes along to help a little bit. Like last year. My American Lit teacher was teaching Emerson's "Self-Reliance." Most of my classmates went glassy-eyed, but not me. I like the way he writes about trusting yourself, about knowing what you are and listening to your heart. I sat there as my teacher read the line "Trust thyself. Every heart vibrates to that iron string" and knew. It was November, windy outside, and tiny ice pellets clicked against the classroom window, but those words felt like July. I remember thinking, That's it—I'm a damn good ballplayer. I'm gay. Deal with it, world.

Of course, things are never that simple. Like the Christmas when I was seven. It was mostly like any other Christmas. We went to church at midnight on Christmas Eve, set out goodies for Santa, drank hot chocolate topped with whipped cream, and woke up early to open presents. The holidays were one of the few times my dad actually there more than just physically. He knelt right down on the floor, pulled a brightly wrapped box from beneath the Christmas tree, and handed it to me. His smile was beautiful as the lights on the tree threw tiny starburst patterns across his face. "Check out the tag," he said as I took the package from him. Instead of the usual "Santa" or "Mom & Dad," I saw "*From: Dad.*" He'd never done anything like that before. I ripped the paper from the box and found a custom uniform, modeled after my dad's own home duds—the same bright white fabric, the same pinstripes, the miniature fitted wool cap, the works.

I acted the way you might expect a seven year-old boy with a major leaguer for a dad to act—I jumped out of my pajamas and into the uniform, tugged down the brim of the cap, and dashed through the living room as if trying to stretch a single into a double. I felt my face grow red and I slapped a high five to my dad as I slid into the tangle of torn wrapping paper and ribbons at the foot of his chair. Safe at home.

I stayed in the uniform as we finished opening the other gifts. My dad sat in his chair taking it in with a satisfied look on his face. Then I wandered over to my older sister Stephie and asked if I could play with her and her stuff. What the hell did I know? I just wanted to play with my older sister, right? She told me to grab my Evel Knievel figure so that I could play house with her. I was changing Malibu Barbi's outfit when I looked up at my dad. The look was gone. He set a half-eaten cookie on the end table by his chair and went outside to shovel snow.

Okay. Imagining the hypothetical interview may have been a bit much. My dad probably wouldn't really call me "flaming homo," but I know he'd be disappointed, just like I now realize his disappointment that Christmas morning. On some level, I want to tell him, to have him accept me, to understand that I can still handle hot liners and nasty breaking stuff. And I do feel for him. Retirement won't be easy. What happens when it's February and he gets the itch but realizes he won't be jetting to Arizona for Spring Training? Forty-one years old and it's time to walk away.

And what's he walking into?

A family in which being a husband and father has been a part-time job ever since he and my mom were married. I know they care about each other, but the fallout from the affair has yet to go away. Somehow I can't picture my mom getting him to take an interest in interior design or French culinary techniques. And Stephanie is more or less out of the picture—a sophomore in college, and she's already told us she won't be coming home next summer. She's stubborn, like him. She also inherited his athletic genes—she's killer on the volleyball court and the softball diamond—but she resented the fact that he hadn't seen her play more than a handful of games all through high school, and not at all since she went to USC on a softball scholarship. Somehow I don't see her encouraging him to re-enter her life. The only mail she ever sends him are postcards of big game animals. She usually writes something like "I hear they're expecting a record hunt in Colorado this year" on the back.

And me. Maybe I'm being too hard on the old guy—maybe I'm not giving him the benefit of the doubt, setting the bar too low. Maybe this news will cause his fathering DNA to kick in. Like Ward Cleaver.

My mom and I are picking him up at the airport soon—she's bringing me along because "sooner is better." Maybe she's right. Maybe once we've tossed his travel bag in the trunk of the Mercedes, taken our places in the car, and merged onto the interstate, I'll say, "Hey, Dad …I've got to tell you something." And maybe he'll look back over his shoulder at me. Having heard my tone of voice, he'll put on a look of fatherly concern, raise an eyebrow, and say, "Sounds like something's bothering you, son—shoot." And just maybe, when I stop stammering and tell him who Justin Steele really is…maybe those movie star wrinkles at the corners of his eyes will bunch up as he smiles knowingly and says, "Hey, champ—that doesn't mean you're not my boy, right?" And then he'll reach back, smiling, and lightly punch my knee as the digital glow of the dashboard charges the air with a magic we can almost feel, washes his face with a light that softens his features, that makes him look less like a Greek god and more like a twenty-first century Ward Cleaver, ready to stand by his boy against the Eddie Haskells of the world.

But I can't shake the feeling that Beav's going to have to go it alone this time.

Jerry

My name is Nathan P. Davidson and I am, or more accurately was, a major league baseball player—a southpaw with enough moxie to wrangle a contract for each of the last twelve seasons. But when I signed my final contract with a perpetually cellar-dwelling American League club (a team my agent and lawyer have advised me to avoid actually naming here), I did so intending to enjoy the perks that come along with being a professional athlete. My wife, bless her trusting soul, had started talking about children that off-season, and I was, quite frankly, not exactly feeling up to the task of completely settling down just yet—I may have been pushing the big four-oh, but on most days, I still felt like a youngster—Rafael Palmeiro may have needed the little blue miracles, but that was never a problem for me. And in addition to that, I intended to gather material for the novel I wanted to write when I retired.

A *novel*? you're thinking. *From an ex-jock?* I can understand your skepticism. You probably expect the kind of formulaic mamby-pamby churned out by the former NFL offensive lineman who passes himself off as a writer of taut psychological thrillers. You should know, however, that while it's true that I can scratch, adjust my cup, and bed the annies with the best of them, I'm not the type to go looking for spots on Miller Lite commercials or to open a steakhouse and attempt to live off what precious little rep I have. Nathan P. Davidson has a little gray matter. When I was in college, my Senior Thesis explored the role of baseball in American Literature. I know that Walt Whitman had written about the game while serving as a newspaper editor in Brooklyn, that F. Scott Fitzgerald added verisimilitude (how's that for a word from a jock) to his short stories by mentioning the Yankees teams of the 1920s and the infamous Black Sox Scandal, that Ernest Hemingway had devoted several pages of *The Old Man and the Sea* to "the great DiMaggio." Phillip Roth had written a baseball novel entitled, interestingly, *The Great American Novel*. Robert Coover, W.P. Kinsella, Don DeLillo, Bernard Malamud…the list could go on and on.

I've always seen merit in these writers' works, but none of them truly "got" baseball—at least not the baseball I knew. They either romanticized the game or over-emphasized the darker attractions to which boys in men's bodies are sometimes prone. And my research had shown that none of these writers ever really explored an element of the baseball subculture that, quite honestly, intrigued me—the ballpark employees, the regular joes I came into contact with on a daily basis over the course of my career…the hot dog vendors and clubhouse boys, the concessionaires and groundskeepers, the scoreboard operators.

The novel I hoped to write hinged upon one of these employees. I wanted to tell the tale of a single season in the "life" of a major league baseball team—not one chasing a pennant, not one locked into the cellar, but a typical, middle-of-the-road team. I planned on using multiple narrators—a player, of course, but also a fan, a bench coach, a member of the team's front office, a radio announcer, and, most importantly, a stadium employee.

A scoreboard operator.

That character was the reason I signed with Team X for my final season. The team's ballpark had one of those hand-operated scoreboards next to the home bullpen, the kind that disappeared when the cookie-cutter stadiums started popping up in the 1970s but that have enjoyed a revival in the retro parks they're building these days. On the other side of a short fence in the bullpen, a scoreboard operator posted the scores of games taking place elsewhere around the league, scores relayed to him every half-inning via a bulky black telephone whose ring was equal parts chain saw and wind chime.

As a reliever, I spent plenty of time in the bullpen, time I'd use, I believed, to research Team X's manual scoreboard operator. I pictured a grizzled old man—someone who had spent his entire life working for the ball club, someone who loved the game but owned a healthy dose of cynicism, who distrusted the money and the glam, who had a folksy wisdom and a way of seeing things for what they are, who had the cojones to call a spade a spade. He'd have no problem revealing the true nature of details glossed over or selectively ignored by the novel's other narrators. He'd be wiry, his shoulders permanently hunched over from working for decades in cramped quarters, his eyes locked into a squint from looking out onto the field through his narrow viewing window. He'd make $8.00 an hour but rub elbows with multi-millionaires on a daily basis. I loved the possibilities for developing dramatic irony with my scoreboard operator. I'd already started to think of him as a friend, someone who was there with me through spring training, mentally commenting in his gravelly voice, sounding an awful lot like Burgess Meredith.

The more I thought about my book, the more I knew its plot

couldn't have a happy resolution. I intended to write serious literature. I wanted to hit the universal themes. Love. Betrayal. The loss of innocence. Characters attempting to find relief from the demons that haunt them, but finding that real relief was a much more difficult proposition than they bargained for—that often, something seeming like relief had real consequences in the long run. Serious literature meant defeat or obfuscation, candles being snuffed out, hopes fleeing for points unknown, never to be heard from again. Ever see Faulkner spoon-feed his readers "happily ever after?" Don't forget that old Miss Emily had steel gray hair, my friend.

I deliberately mention Faulkner here because he immediately came to mind when I met Team X's scoreboard operator for the first time. More accurately, perhaps I should say that one of Faulkner's characters came to mind. The operator wasn't gnarled, didn't have permanently stooped shoulders, didn't talk in a gravelly voice. He did, however, like Faulkner's Benjie Compson, live with a disability.

He had cerebral palsy.

In these pages, I'll call him Jerry, as legal cases involving members of his family, Team X, and a certain Legend who once played for Team X has yet to be resolved in the courts (gratuitous if you ask me, but if a buck's to be made, why not take up America's other great pastime—litigation?). I first met Jerry on Opening Day. I had made my way to the bullpen with the other relievers after the player introductions and found a spot on the end of the bullpen bench, nearest Jerry's working area. His quarters, as I'd expected, were cramped and dark, but I could make him out working at the other end of the enclosure, shuffling the two-foot square wooden shingles with stark white numbers painted beneath the grommetted holes he slipped over rusted metal hooks, hanging them to display the score. I leaned over the low fence and called out to get his attention. "Hey, bud," I said in my best ballplayer lingo. I introduced myself and asked, "How's it hangin' over there?"

The worker moved clumsily through the shadows toward the bullpen. It wasn't until he was about ten feet away that I saw him clearly for the first time. He flashed a wide, wet grin, and in a strained voice that seemed stuck somewhere between his throat and nose, he said, "Hi, Mr. Davidson."

I was shocked—both by his condition and at the recognition. To my eye, he seemed almost ageless—equal parts Yoda from *Star Wars* and McCauly Culkin in *Home Alone*. His eyes were heavy-lidded, and his facial features were soft and looked as though the sculptor who'd carved them hadn't finished the job. I stuttered a bit before I managed to speak. "You know the game if you recognize me just like that."

"I love baseball," he said. He didn't really pronounce the "s" in baseball (the word sounded like "*baahbawl*"), and as he spoke I could see a string of saliva stretching away from his bottom lip—but not quite breaking free and falling down over his chin. "I know every player in both leagues," he said. He wiped the string of saliva from his bottom lip with the back of his hand and continued. "I have a *com-pyhuter*, and I go to the Internet to all the *baahbawl* sites." He started rattling off the names of players, statistics, uniform numbers, and biographical material that left my head spinning.

My stomach lurched as I mentally grasped for an appropriate response. Early in my career, as part of a charity program sponsored by the United Way, I'd visited a recreation center for the disabled. It had creeped me out—lots of grunting and squeaking, walkers scraping over the tiled floor with an odd locomotion as their users struggled to keep themselves upright, the scent of full diapers seeming to follow me wherever I went. I swore that I'd never go back. But now...my wizened narrator seemed to have hopped a train for parts unknown.

Jerry must have sensed my discomfort, because he tossed me a line. "It's okay, Mr. Davidson—what I've got isn't con*t-haaaay*-gious." He laughed, his very pink tongue lolling out from the corner of his mouth.

"What do you mean?" I asked, jamming my hands into the pockets of my warm-up jacket. I noticed that I'd inched down the bench away from Jerry.

"You just look fr-*heaked* out, like if I said 'boo,' you'd run away. I have cerebral *p-hallsy*, that's all," he said. Few of his words contained clean, closing articulations.

I removed my hands from the pockets of my warm-up jacket, and forced myself to straighten my posture. He was sharp. "I'm sorry," I said. "It's just...I didn't mean to..."

"I know," he said. "I've made worse first impr-*hessssions*." I felt my cheeks flushing, and I would have liked to crawl beneath the bench in the bullpen. "At least you talked to me," Jerry said. He craned his neck to look past me down the bench. "Some guys are real *aah-hu-ooooles*," he said. "They won't even look at me."

My mind was no longer reeling, and suddenly, a new vision of my critical narrator started to emerge. I looked him over, smiled, and asked him his name. He introduced himself.

"Well, Jerry," I said, "the only assholes down here are the ones we sit on." I extended my hand across the low fence and we shook. That's when I first noticed another of Jerry's distinguishing physical qualities—his unbalanced physical development. His right arm and leg were much smaller than their counterparts on the left. To return to my earlier sculpture metaphor, it seemed as though Jerry had been only partially formed—thick wet clay over a wire frame. I never saw Jerry actually use his right arm (either in his job or in the tasks that he so willingly carried out for my compadres in the bullpen). The condition of his right leg gave him a peculiar way of moving; if you listened carefully to him as he walked, you could detect a rhythm in the pattern of right foot-drag and left foot-step, a sort of syncopation at once playful and labored. Jerry's left arm, however, was magnificent. His bicep bulged beneath the thin cotton t-shirts he wore to the park most days, and the tendons and muscles of his forearm looked like twisted bands of steel beneath his skin.

When I lay in bed that night, reflecting on that first meeting, I thought of Jerry's smile, his unfinished facial features, his imprecise articulation, his massive arm. I remembered an article I'd read about Hemingway's years in Bermuda, how one of his arms became noticeably larger than the other from battling marlins and sharks he hooked while out on his fishing boat, how after docking his boat he would chalk off a square on the pier, plunk down $100, and declare that anyone who could defeat him in bare-knuckle boxing could walk off with his money. No one ever took the $100, though. Hemingway would take the blows of any challenger, waiting for his opportunity to land one good punch with his overdeveloped arm. And typically, one good punch was all it took to send his challenger away with a nose gushing blood, an eye swollen shut, or ears ringing with an unnatural tintinnabulation. Hemingway loved it.

Through my actions as a sort of advocate, Jerry came to love all of us, and the affection eventually became mutual. My teammates especially came to value Jerry after he put his massive arm to use for purposes other than hanging numbers on the scoreboard. The bullpen is its own world, nothing like the dugout or even the clubhouse, where the relievers have one thing in large measure—time. And time, of course, must be occupied. You've probably seen some bullpen footage during the blooper reels they play on the Jumbotrons between innings—pitcher A giving pitcher B a hot-foot, pitcher C biting his nails down to the first knuckle, pitcher D drawing pictures (typically perverted, though the cameraman never catches that) in the dirt with the business end of a bat. One way we occupied time that season was gorging ourselves—on hot dogs and bratwurst slathered in red sauce, on peanuts in the shell and doughy pretzels with cups of yellow-orange cheese sauce for dipping, ice cream scooped into miniature batting helmet bowls, nachos spilling over the edges of cardboard trays, and sweating cups of watered-down Pepsi. And it was Jerry who smuggled the contraband from the nearest concession stand.

Skeptical? Asking yourself, "What about the bullpen coach who's there to monitor warm-ups and babysit?" As my teammates put it that season, they "had 'Ol Sully by the short hairs"—the result of his having been found in a compromising position with a self-employed model during spring training. Sully's wife didn't find out so long as certain things were understood in the bullpen. We weren't about to contend for a pennant (we were fifteen games out of first by Memorial Day), and the general make-up of our pen believed in the old school of athletic training—if hot dogs, brews, and heaters had worked for the Bambino, who were we to argue? You might also note that the composite earned run average of our bullpen climbed each month of the season—one of only two clubs to share such a dubious honor.

Jerry's ability to get us food never ceased to amaze. Hernandez, an especially portly right-hander who, like me, had reached the end of the line, would empty a large, orange Gatorade cooler as we took up a collection, and then we'd send Jerry on his way. Within minutes (Jerry was very conscientious about his primary job, after all) he would return with the cooler crammed full of highly caloric—but very tasty—ballpark fare, the cooler atop his left shoulder, propped up with and balanced by that remarkable left arm of his.

But aside from the food, we all had our reason for loving Jerry. Finley liked to think himself quite the vocalist, and Jerry was the only person who would compliment his tone-deaf renditions of Broadway show tunes. Vizcaino was a real gearhead, so Jerry would bring in muscle car magazines and allow himself to be lectured on the finer points of the big block engines GM dropped into its performance vehicles in the 1960s. And the rookie Powell was, to put it mildly, one awfully horny dude; he enjoyed an activity he liked to refer to as "beaver hunting"—watching the young women in short skirts and halter-tops who often sat in bleachers doing their best Sharon Stone impersonations. Powell would scribble notes—usually names of clubs where they could meet him after the game—and send Jerry into the stands to deliver them. Jerry would also dutifully return whatever these women would send back—phone numbers written in large, round letters on department store receipts, tissues bearing the soft imprint of lipstick, lewd allusions to what they considered their best assets, and, on one memorable occasion, a Victoria's Secret bra that smelled faintly of tulips.

So you're probably thinking, *Christ, you sure got the mileage out of the poor stooge*, but I'd have to disagree with that perspective. If I were the cynical type, I could argue that we'd resurrected one of baseball's oldest traditions, a custom abandoned in this age of political correctness—that Jerry had become our mascot. I know—when you watch baseball games, you see furry "mascots." But creations like the "Phillie Phanatic" or the "San Diego Chicken" pale by comparison to the mascots major league clubs had some decades ago. Today's puffballs are the brainchild of some mid-level manager in the front office who decided to use his marketing degree to "Disney-fy" the ballpark and attract a new generation of fans. But take a look at your baseball history—watch the early innings of Ken Burns' *Baseball*, or read biographies of the greats of the game's earlier era. You'll find that teams used to keep mascots right in the dugout. These mascots were typically freaks of humanity—hunchbacks, midgets, mongoloids, and the like—and players often rubbed them for good luck before stepping to the plate or taking their position in the field. John McGraw, the Giants' great manager, used to train his team's mascot, a hunchback, to steal the other team's signs and to get under the skin of the opposing team's players by performing grossly exaggerated pantomimes of their performance on the field.

Yes, it is true that the part of Jerry that loved the game may have done almost anything we asked, but we also felt a genuine affection for him. We supplemented his paltry hourly wage with generous tips. We passed along autographed balls and photos. And there was that off-day during a July home stand when we took Jerry out to one of our favorite watering holes (an incident my agent advises against detailing at this time, but let me say with confidence that Jerry was smiling by night's end). We were, in Jerry's words, his "best boys."

Late in the season, we even had special t-shirts printed; they bore Jerry's likeness along with the inscription "I'm one of Jerry's kids!" He was genuinely moved the day when, during the seventh inning stretch, we all went to the short fence separating his workspace from the bullpen and opened our jerseys to reveal the t-shirts. Jerry began to cry and called us the "best friends anyone could ever ask *fuh-oooor*." Eight Fruit of the Loom, pre-shunk, 100 percent cotton t-shirts: $40; design and printing charge at local t-shirt emporium: $115; look on Jerry's face upon seeing all of us wearing a picture of him across our chests: priceless. It was the least we could do.

And when Jerry died that crisp October afternoon, we cried real tears.

It happened on the last day of the season, one of those afternoons when soft white clouds piled upon themselves in contrast with the sharp blue of the sky. Team X, interestingly, had a sell-out crowd that day—certainly not because of our exploits on the field, but because it was to be the final game ever played in the stadium. Team X would move into a lush, state-of-the-art baseball emporium the following season, one full of luxury boxes and digital replay screens (though it would have a manual scoreboard for that "retro" effect—a scoreboard which, we all assumed, would be manned by Jerry). Fifty thousand fans had come to say good-bye to the stadium that had been the team's home for decades. Predictably, we lost by a score of 7 to 2, but the fans remained in the stands for a special post-game ceremony in which former players (many of them from a time when Team X was not the perpetual doormat they'd become in recent years) appeared once more. Jerry watched the ceremony through the viewing window in the outfield wall. We'd come to find out that Jerry had been working for Team X in some capacity for over a decade. Having been a part of some of those sunnier years, Jerry, too, was swept up in nostalgia of cheering former home run champions and Cy Young Award winners as they trotted across the diamond one last time. He began stomping his one good leg along with the fans in the bleachers above him as they roared for The Legend who'd recently been inducted into the Baseball Hall of Fame. And as the roar crescendoed, as the stamping's intensity increased, the rafters supporting the bleachers literally began to vibrate with accumulated love.

In early September, when he found out The Legend would be participating in the ceremony, Jerry confessed that The Legend had been his all-time favorite player. Jerry told me how when The Legend would make a catch deep in the outfield to end the inning, he would trot along the warning track, past Jerry's window, and toss him the ball through the opening. When I asked him if he'd liked The Legend even better than me and my mates in the bullpen, he blushed and stammered and didn't know what to say. I told him it was okay, that I wouldn't tell anyone else. He seemed relieved, then laughed and squeezed me with his powerful arm, nearly causing me to cough up the piece of contraband bratwurst.

On that October day, I watched Jerry, lost in his reverie, his head tilted slightly to better see the field. I couldn't help but smile at the warmth of the fans—and at the prospects of my post-baseball plans and how fortune had given me a model for one of my novel's narrators superior to any I could have ever imagined myself—and watched as The Legend stood near second base. Someone handed him a ball and a pen. Carefully, deliberately, he signed the ball and blew the ink dry. Holding the ball high above his head, he turned slowly, counter-clockwise, as if he wanted to etch the scene indelibly in his mind, to bathe one last time in the collective voice of the assembled crowd. As he began his slow turn toward the outfield, I could tell his eyes had locked on Jerry's window. He made a tossing motion toward left field. The fans in the bleachers screamed, thinking that his gesture meant he would hurl the treasured ball into their midst—the ultimate souvenir of their attendance at that final game in the former home of Team X. I knew better.

What a beautiful gesture, I thought. As The Legend crow-stepped into his throw, I actually felt a lump rise in my throat and knew that the goose bumps along my arms weren't from the day's chilly temperature. The ball flew toward left field spinning in a high arc. Fans near the fence jockeyed for position and held out gloves and caps, hoping to snare the horsehide sphere from the air, but they didn't have a chance. The ball's angle of descent carried it directly toward Jerry's window.

I saw Jerry's gentle smile—he'd watched enough games to be able to judge trajectory. He backed away from the window, as he knew he wouldn't be able to catch the ball. He must have planned to let it come through, to strike the floor of his workspace and bounce to a stop before seizing it. The ball, though, caught the edge of the open window and ricocheted at an odd angle. Awkwardly, Jerry turned away and threw up his one good hand. It wasn't enough. The ball struck his temple, then fell to the floor and rolled beneath a folding chair.

Jerry fell face-first, landing on his stomach. We all hopped the fence and ran to his side, but there was nothing we could do—he didn't breathe, hadn't even twitched. His head was twisted to one side, his mouth forming a crooked "o", and his heavy-lidded eyes were half-open. A single thread of blood trickled from his ear, forming a pool no bigger than a half-dollar on the concrete. And as the fans continued cheering the ceremony on the field (and as The Legend, oblivious, pointed to Jerry's window, smiled, and flashed a "thumbs up"), we summoned medical assistance over the bullpen phone.

As we waited for the paramedics who would tell us what we already knew in our hearts, we said our good-byes to Jerry. Hernandez tucked a five-dollar bill into the back pocket of his jeans. Powell placed a phone number alongside the five-spot and told him to "look her up some time." Finley began humming quietly, and for the first time, no one told him to shut up.

I walked to Jerry's folding chair and picked up the ball. I squinted through the tears and read the inscription on the ball: "To Jerry, Good luck in your new digs! 'The Legend.'" Jerry had fallen on top of his good arm, so I gently pulled it out from under him and opened his hand. I placed the ball on his palm and closed his still-warm fingers around the ball.

The Scorebook

Simon was one of those geek-nerds with Coke bottle glasses and high-waisted polyester pants off the clearance rack at K-Mart. To be perfectly honest, I hassled him as much as anyone else did—probably more during the baseball season. Why he bothered going out for the team was beyond me, but there he was, all four years. During practice, Simon begged out of drills, and trying to get him into the batting cage was like giving a cat a bath. His being on the team had more to do with the fact that our school was so small; only a dozen guys went out for the team, and Coach had twenty uniforms. That and his talent with numbers—he kept the scorebook and prepared incredibly detailed statistical breakdowns that impressed the hell out of Coach: pie charts, bar graphs, tables detailing a hitter's performance plotted against variables like barometric pressure—the kind of stuff even the Elias Sports Bureau doesn't have.

For the rest of us, he was useful, too—an easy mark in the locker room, especially for Brett MacArthur, our shortstop and star player. Brett occupied the top rung in the high school pecking order—a good-looking, popular, three-sport athlete who hit the snot out of a baseball and especially enjoyed tormenting Simon (and enlisting anyone above Simon on the ladder to help dole out the punishment). I wouldn't even want to guess how many pairs of Fruit of the Looms we shredded giving him wedgies or the number of times we crammed him into the dumpster behind the bus garage and sat on the lid until he stopped begging to be let out.

So when things went down the way they did at Senior Prom, no one saw it coming. I was standing with Brett MacArthur and the rest of the Prom Court in the back of the gym. We were having pictures taken for the yearbook and waiting for the Grand March to begin when Brett nudged me and tipped his head toward the D.J. at the opposite end of the gym. There was Simon, standing by the giant stacks of speakers and lighting rigs looking rather different, even for him. He wore the kind of pastel blue *Miami Vice*-style suit that popped up in the "Prom Special" copies of *Seventeen* the girls leafed through behind their copies of *America in Literature* in Mrs. Lucht's class—glossy magazines where model-perfect girls and their hunky dates (who all looked vaguely like Kirk Cameron) stepped out of limousines and dashed through a sea of balloons. In a small town like Gillett, none of us had the nerve to wear anything but the standard tux with cummerbund and bow tie matching our dates' dresses. A pick-up with holes rusted in the floorboards was considered good wheels, and if you could score an old conversion van with curtains over the windows, well, you were a hot commodity.

Simon had left his shirt unbuttoned almost to his belly—the endless lights reflected from the mirror ball crawled across his chest, highlighting ugly acne scars—and all night, he'd been clutching a blue-covered spiral-bound notebook, a baseball scorekeeper's book. I watched him conduct what looked like heated negotiations with the D.J. They each gestured wildly and were shouting at each other, though I couldn't hear any of it over the throb of the music, and money finally changed hands. The D.J. handed Simon a microphone and began shuffling through a box of tapes. He pulled one out, showed it to Simon, who gave him a thumbs-up, and put it into a tape deck as the final notes of vintage 80's dance pop bounced around the gym. Simon let the echoes die before he spoke. "Hey there," he said, forcing his voice into a much lower register than I was used to hearing from him. He didn't look comfortable, but he went on, still holding onto the scorebook. "You know, this is a really big night, a night for love." He drew out the "o" in "love," letting his voice drop even lower as he did.

Brett turned to our group. "New soap-on-a-rope?" he said, then cupped his hand, grabbed the crotch of his pants, and made a quick jerking motion. Everyone laughed.

Simon continued. "A night for new…possibilities. To honor these 'possibilities,' I've prepared a special musical number for you. This one especially goes out to Kristin Hanson." He waved the scorebook in her direction. "Hit it, maestro."

Those who weren't hooting stood there with their jaws hanging open. Simon may as well have slit his wrists. Kristin Hanson was hands-down the most beautiful girl in the school—a package of curves, blonde hair, and ice blue eyes. She made anything male weak in the knees—and she was Brett MacArthur's girlfriend. At first she looked as though she was about to cough up what little she'd eaten of her pre-Prom dinner, but the look that soon turned to embarrassment as she flushed red even through her fake-n-bake tan. The D.J. hit the play button and the sick-sweet string opening of the theme song to *The Love Boat* came through the speakers. Simon, in a voice uncomfortably situated somewhere between Wayne Newton and Neil Diamond, launched into the vocal. "Love… exciting and new. Come aboard…"

Brett, his fist clenched, made a move toward Simon, but Kristin grabbed him by the arm and held him back. "What the—" Brett said, "you telling me you actually *like* this?"

"No," Kristin said, her face still red, "but what are you going to do? Punch him out? And then what? Huggy Bear hauls you into the cop shop? Come on—we're the ones with the room tonight, right?" She ran her fingers over the silky lapels of his jacket, but she didn't look at him.

Brett stared at Huggy Bear, the grossly overweight cop who'd drawn Prom duty. He stood by the refreshment table, guarding the punch bowl and scarfing down miniature cream puffs. Brett unclenched his fists, and the tension seemed to drain out of him. Then he looked at me, smiling, and said, "Locker room, Monday, after practice—the little shit won't know what hit him."

I didn't say a word. As I watched Simon up there, something gave way inside me—what he was doing serious cojones. He was really giving it up, and he finally found a schmaltzy groove that would have made any lounge singer proud. And in all honesty, who could have blamed Simon? There wasn't a guy in the entire school who hadn't fantasized about Kristin Hanson at some point. When he went into the final line of the song—"Welcome aboard, it's love"—he looked back at Kristin, grinned, and, though I can't be sure given the lighting, winked at her. Kristin gathered the folds of her skirt and whirled away from the dance floor, the satin of her floor-length dress swooshing as she left the gym.

After practice Monday, Brett looked at me with that gleam in his eye that he saved for moments like this, but I shook my head. "Sorry," I said, shoving my mitt into my equipment bag.

"What?" he said. "Are you nuts?"

Simon was sitting on the bench three lockers down from me, watching. He didn't move.

"What good would it do? We graduate in a month and a half, and you'll never have to see him again." I looked to Simon and asked, "Where are you going to college?"

"Yale," he said.

I looked back to Brett. I knew he was going to Oshkosh, or UW-"0" as one of our cynical teachers referred to it. "Sheesh, bro—from the way you're acting, a person might think you're…" I let my voice trail off, not yet ready to say what my mind had formulated.

Brett narrowed his eyes. "It's about justice, plain and simple, asshole."

I didn't press the issue. Brett was steaming, especially after the rumor had gone around school that once he and Kristin got to the hotel room, she couldn't stop talking about how Simon had sung for her and asked why Brett never did anything like that. Depending upon the version of the story you heard, she demanded that Brett sing "Up Where We Belong" or "Wind Beneath My Wings," and when he refused, she put the kibosh on things fast. Brett became angry, and Kristin left.

Brett glared at me. "So are you with me or what?"

I didn't move.

"Fine." He brushed past me and grabbed Simon by his shirt. Simon didn't stand a chance. Thirty seconds later, the waistband of Simon's underwear had been stretched up and over his head, what Brett called "The Nuclear Wedgie." He shoved him into an empty locker, leaving Simon's arms and legs poking awkwardly out from the steel cage. Brett stormed out the locker room, the sound of his shouted profanities echoing off the tile floor.

I held out my hand and helped Simon extract himself from the narrow opening of the locker. "You okay?" I asked.   He nodded after managing to slip the waistband down from around his head. He tentatively stepped away from the wall of lockers, inhaled deeply, and bent over double. I heard him mutter what a bastard under his breath.

"I know what you mean," I said.

After that day, a sort of unspoken understanding existed between Simon and me. He didn't ask why I didn't stop things in the locker room—he understood certain things—but he thanked me in the hallway after school the next day for not having helped Brett.

We played Oconto Falls two weeks later. We expected to be eaten alive by the Panthers—they had a pitcher named Bob Watham who would go on to a ten-year major league career as a relief pitcher for a number of teams. As we left the bus, Brett shoved past Simon, pushing him back into his seat, and hissed, "Chickenshit." The #2 Dixon Ticonderoga that Simon typically kept tucked eraser end first under the sweatband of his cap fell to the floor.

Simon stood up, straightened his glasses, and mumbled something I couldn't understand. He grabbed the scorebook from the bus seat, picked up his pencil, and made his way to the visiting team's dugout.

When we came up to bat in the first, I glanced at Simon in his usual spot at he end of the bench, scorebook open on his lap, pencil in hand. He noticed me looking at him, and with his head, he motioned me to join him. I slid toward the end of the bench. "Watch and learn," he said.

Our leadoff hitter, Jimmy Cole, stepped into the batters box. I didn't envy his position—I imagined that his knees were knocking the way mine would when my spot in the order came up. Simon licked the tip of his pencil and placed it in the box that would detail Jimmy's at-bat in the scorebook, but before Watham ever threw his first pitch, Simon circled the faint blue "1B" that indicated a single and drew a diagonal line from home to first on the tiny schematic in the box. Watham threw two strikes to Jimmy—heaters that I swore I heard hissing even from the dugout—then tried to waste a pitch that hung just a bit too close to the plate. Jimmy swung and sent a looping line drive over the second baseman's head for a clean single.

Before Watham's first pitch to our number two hitter, Scott DeBauch, Simon again placed his pencil in Jimmy's box, drawing a line from first to second and printing the letters "SB" above second. I watched Coach in the third base coach's box going through a series of signals to Scott and then to Jimmy. He flashed Jimmy the steal sign, and on Watham's first pitch, Jimmy broke for second. The Panthers' catcher had difficulty picking the ball out of his mitt, delaying his throw by a fraction of a second. Jimmy was safe, and as he stood on the bag brushing dirt from his pants, I saw Simon draw the line showing him going from second to third, saw Simon circle "1B" and draw the line to first in Scott DeBauch's box.

Watham's next offering to Scott was a message pitch, flying straight toward his shoulder. To avoid being hit, Scott bailed. Miraculously, his bat followed his body and intercepted the pitch. The ball sailed toward the hole between second and third, landing on the outfield grass just out of the reach of the Panthers' shortstop. Scott scrambled back to his feet and went to first; Jimmy not wanting to be doubled off had the shortstop caught the ball, stayed close to the bag, but as soon as the ball hit the grass, he took off for third and safely slid into the base.

I looked at Simon and asked, "How did you—"

71

He shook his head. "Not now," he said. "Don't interrupt me."

Runners on the corners, nobody out, and Brett was our next hitter. Simon extended Scott's line to second base, and in Brett's box, drew the diagonal from home to first and printed the letters "HBP." *Damn*, I thought, *he's out for blood*.

Brett kicked at the dirt in the batter's box like a bull and spit violently into the dust. He took Watham's first pitch for strike one. Watham's second pitch was a curveball that just missed the outside corner. Brett swung at the third pitch and sent a foul ball screaming into the Panthers' dugout, where players scattered as the ball wiped out a water cooler. Brett snickered and knocked the dirt from his cleats with the nob end of his bat. He stepped back into the box and wagged his bat at Watham.

Even from the dugout, I could see that the next pitch somehow defied every law of physics I'd ever been taught. The ball appeared headed low and well outside, but just before reaching the catcher, it sharply swept up and in—catching Brett in the crotch with a sickening thwack that echoed off the aluminum bleachers. He went down like a bag of cement and began squirming in slow motion in the dirt. Watham looked sick—he clearly hadn't intended the ball to behave as it had—and Coach rushed to the plate. Eventually, Brett managed to get to his hands and knees, but when he tried to stand up, he vomited. Chunks of lunchroom pizza splashed in the dirt.

Next to me on the bench, Simon laughed to himself and whispered "Touché, asshole." I felt sick watching Brett finally get to his feet and stumble to the dugout, and I reached down to adjust my protective cup. Coach sent Will Nelson into the game for Brett; and the Panthers' coach hauled a bag of sand and a rake out to the plate to clean up Brett's lunch.

I looked at Simon. "What's going—"

"I told you not to interrupt me, not now. Just watch." His eyes seemed cloudy and distant behind his thick glasses. He looked back down at the scorebook and in the first box next to our clean-up hitter, Lance Frank, he penciled in a "K." Frank struck out on three pitches. As our number five hitter, Jeff Wilke, made his way to the plate, I grabbed my bat and helmet and started for the on-deck circle. "Wait one second," Simon said. "Watch."

Simon penciled in a "K" in the first inning box corresponding with Jeff Wilke's place in the order, then moved to my box, circled the blue letters "HR," traced and filled in the diamond formed by his lines—a grand slam home run. *Not off Watham*, I thought. "Oh, yes—off Watham," said Simon.

I pulled on a batting helmet. "Trust me," Simon said as I walked up the dugout steps. Wilke struck out on three pitches, and I felt as though I would be sick. I'd played ball against Watham going back to Little League, and in all the times I'd faced him, the best I'd ever managed was a weak infield single that could have just as easily been ruled an error by the official scorer. It was Watham who, during the Babe Ruth League season the summer before my freshman year, threw me the first real curveball I'd ever seen and effectively ended any dreams I'd had about one day becoming a major leaguer.

Watham couldn't hide his grin as I walked to the plate. I knew exactly what he was thinking as I stepped into the box, and I tried not to mess myself as I imagined what must be running through his head. I went into my stance, half swung my bat as he looked in toward his catcher, and then closed my eyes and swallowed hard as he went into his motion. I heard the shotgun explosion of the ball as it slammed into the catcher's mitt, heard the umpire call out, "Ball one."

I opened my eyes and saw Watham chuckle. He looked back at me and mouthed words at me over the top of his glove. I didn't want to think about what they might be. I just felt a cold trickle of sweat over my ribs and looked to Coach standing in the box outside third base, running through a series of signs. He brushed his left forearm to wipe out the first sequence, then brushed his right thigh, telling me to take the next pitch. *No argument here*, I thought. Watham's second pitch was also a ball, as was his third, and I could tell he was not happy. He bounced the rosin bag over his pitching hand, then hurled it to the ground, sending a red cloud up from the dirt of the mound. He no longer smiled; instead he glared at me with a look that would've stripped wallpaper. Coach again flashed the take sign. I didn't see any problem with his logic. A walk would put us on the board.

I saw Simon in the dugout, still sitting at the end of the bench. He traced circles in the air on a horizontal plane with the eraser end of his pencil, mimicking the movement of runners around the base. *He's crazy*, I thought. I didn't even bother fully going into my batting stance as Watham rocked into his motion—I stood straight, my bat resting on my back shoulder, but as soon as the ball left Watham's hand, I felt myself lurch involuntarily. I had no control over my front foot as it rose and stepped in perfect rhythm, no control over my arms as they pulled back my hands slightly into the hitch that served as my mechanism to begin what was a textbook swing, my left shoulder remaining closed, my left elbow close to my ribs as my right arm steered the bat through the strike zone. The collision of bat and ball sent the sweet shock of perfect contact back up through my arms and created an aluminum *ping* more beautiful than any I'd ever heard. For a moment, I stood there stupidly, watching the ball as it soared over the fence in left-center. The entire team greeted me at home plate with high fives and back slaps—except Brett, who sat at one end of the dugout bench, moving as little as possible, and Simon, who sat at the other end of the bench, elbows on knees, looking down at Brett with the biggest shit-eating grin I'd ever seen.

I pulled off my batting helmet and asked Simon, "What just happened here?"

Simon pulled off his glasses. For a moment, he looked like a deer in the headlights—frantic, frozen, wanting to run but not able to make a break. He squinted at the lenses, and wiped them against his pants.

"Come on," I said. I could still feel the sweet shock of bat on ball tingling back through my arms, could still see Simon marking the home run in my square, and I imagined just how sweet the rest of the season could be. "Don't you think you owe me a little something after the other day?"

"That wasn't enough?" Simon nodded toward the field where Watham had just struck out the next hitter on three pitches.

"Look, we both know I'm on your side in this thing." For the first time ever, I heard myself trying to butter up Simon. "You're sure you couldn't just…?"

Simon put his glasses back on and sighed. "Meet me in the locker room before school tomorrow," he said under his breath. "But none of this—*none* of it—ever gets out."

Even at 7:30 in the morning, the air in the locker room was thick with the smell of sweat and decaying steel, of damp gym shorts and the fuzzy mold that grew in one corner of the shower. I saw the light was on in Coach's office and heard the whir of his copy machine, so I popped in and say hello before finding Simon. To my surprise, it was Simon. "Hey," I said.

Simon lifted the lid of the copier and flipped something on the glass. "Hey," he said, looking back at me briefly. I couldn't detect anything in his look.

I leaned against the filing cabinet. "No Coach?"

Simon pushed a button on the machine. "He went to the lounge for coffee." From beneath the slightly raised lid of the copier, I saw the slow crawl of the light beneath the glass. "Probably won't be back until the beginning of first hour—"

I interrupted him. "Look, Simon, I don't know how you did whatever you did yesterday, but I wanted to say thanks and was wondering if you might—"

"It wasn't me," Simon blurted. He held his hands in front of him awkwardly, as if he didn't know what to do with them.

"Wasn't you?" I asked. "But I saw what you did—you had it all down in the scorebook before it ever happened. I watched you mark my homer before I ever went to the on-deck circle!"

Simon sighed, went to the large window of Coach's office, and looked out into the locker room. "Close the door," he said. I didn't question him. He went to the copier, gathered a thin sheaf of papers from the tray, and opened the cover. He pulled out a blue-covered scorekeeper's book from his backpack and set it on Coach's desk. "Do you know who Russ Hodges is?"

Even in high school, I knew my baseball. "Of course," I said. "*The Giants win the pennant!* The radio announcer for the Giants, 1951, it's him calling Thomson's 'Shot Heard 'Round the World' in the playoff against Brooklyn."

Simon arched an eyebrow. He removed his glasses and wiped them with the untucked tail of his shirt. Squinting at me, he asked, "Did you know he's my great uncle?"

It was my turn to be impressed. "You're shitting me, right?"

He put his glasses back on. "It's the truth. Here," he said, picking up the scorekeeper's book and flipping through the pages. He stopped several pages away from the end of the spiral-bound book and held it open, exposing two pages that had started turning yellow at their edges, and handed the book to me. "Take a look at this."

I scanned the pages. The pencil markings were faint but still legible, and in flashes, the information came to me—Location: Polo Grounds; Date: October 3, 1951. I looked over the top page—a line-up for the Brooklyn Dodgers, and penciled in at the bottom of the page was the pitcher, Ralph Branca. On the bottom page, the New York Giants' line-up—and there was Bobby Thomson, third base. I placed the tip of my index finger on his name, and barely touching the paper, traced the line of boxes to the right. There, in the last inning, I saw it: the darkened square, the circled letters "HR"—the Shot Heard 'Round the World! "Oh my God!" I said.

Simon smiled, somewhat smugly.

"How'd you get this?" I asked. "Shouldn't this be in the Baseball Hall of Fame or—"

"I told you," Simon said, "Russ Hodges was my dad's uncle. This is the scorebook he kept in the booth October 3, 1951—didn't even belong to him until that day. That was the first, and only, game he ever recorded in it." Simon scratched the side of his nose. "A beat writer, an old-timer who covered the Giants for the *Times*, gave it to him. Uncle Russ had used the last entry in his book the day before and went to the press room to see if he could bum a scorebook from somebody. He was asking around when the beat writer overheard him and pulled him aside. 'Here,' he told Uncle Russ, 'use this. It's time for me to pass this along anyway. Used to belong to Frank Graham himself. But you ought to know...'"

Simon went on, relating what the old sportswriter had told his great uncle, that Frank Graham had given *him* the scorebook after the third game in the 1932 World Series between the Yankees and the Cubs. The moment Simon mentioned that, I flipped through the book and found the game. There it was—Charlie Root on the mound for the Cubs, Babe Ruth in the three hole for the Yankees. "Apparently," Simon said, "Frank Graham told this writer that when Ruth called his shot against Root, he started feeling all tingly. Ruth hits the homer, and when Frank Graham marks it in the scorebook, he marks it in Lou Gehrig's box by mistake. But before he could erase it, Gehrig hits a home run too. So Graham tries it for the next hitter as well—he marks a ground out, 6-3— and the batter grounds out to the shortstop."

I felt my jaw drop. "You're telling me," I asked, "that whoever keeps score with this book controls what happens in the game?"

"I wish it were that simple," Simon said. He sat down behind the desk in Coach's beat-up office chair. "The scorebook's power is limited. One-half inning per game—that's all you get."

What he said made sense—after our fast start against Watham the night before, we ended up losing the Oconto Falls game by three runs.

Simon punched buttons on a stopwatch on Coach's desk as he continued. "Uncle Russ didn't believe the beat writer—until Bobby

Thomson comes to bat in the bottom of the ninth. My uncle told my dad he figured, *what the hell*, and marked the homer. Next thing you know, Branca grooves one and the Giants win the pennant. Chalk one up for the history books."

Simon told me that Hodges then gave the scorebook to Simon's father, his godchild, along with a description of the power it held. Simon's father, who was never much of a baseball fan, passed it, and the story, along to Simon when Simon had told him he was going out for baseball Freshman year. Simon, who possessed a healthy measure of his father's skepticism regarding anything not involving equations or the scientific method, told me he hadn't even considered using the scorebook until the day he saw Brett and Kristin at Brett's locker a month before Prom. He'd had a crush on Kristin going back to the eighth grade. That day, he sensed something out of the ordinary going on between Brett and Kristin, so he made himself as inconspicuous as possible, digging through his own locker while eavesdropping on their conversation. They were arguing, and though Simon couldn't make out every word, he did get the context—Brett had made it very clear he expected to cross home plate the night of Prom. Simon decided to take it upon himself to do something about that.

I felt my stomach churning as Simon told me the story and wished I had eaten something for breakfast so my insides would have something to work on other than themselves. And I started to feel dizzy—in one sense, it all sounded so unlikely, but in another way, everything he said rang true. "But where does the scorebook enter into *that*?" I asked and sat down on the other chair in the room. I started flipping through the rest of the scorebook. Room enough for a half-dozen games remained.

Simon placed his hands on the desk, as if he were about to push himself up from his chair. "You'd better give that to me," he said.

I scanned hieroglyphics scribbled onto the scorebook's pages. It contained the complete record of so many of the games I'd read about in the meager collection of baseball books kept in our school library—Johnny Vander Meer's back-to back no-hitters in June of 1938, several games during the course of DiMaggio's 56-game hitting streak, the Red Sox's final game of 1941 when Ted Williams became the last player to hit over .400 for the season.

"I really need that book back," Simon said, reaching across the desk. He was about to take the scorebook from me when I saw IT: a game record like none I'd ever seen, one that was far from being complete—not even out of the top of the first. The home team was listed as "Hanson," the visiting squad "Delzer," Simon's last name.

"What's this?" I asked.

Simon's face became as red as our jerseys. "Please, give it to me now," he said. "You don't need—"

I stood up and stepped away from the desk. "I want to know what this is all about," I said. On the page matching up with his name, he'd entered a line-up that had "Love Boat" scribbled in as the lead-off hitter and ended with "diamond ring in the roses" in the ninth slot. In the first inning box for "Love Boat," he'd circled 1B and drawn a diagonal line to first base. "A single?"

The color left Simon's face. He placed his elbows on the desk, propped his head in his hands, and muttered, "No one's supposed to know about that."

I looked from the scorebook to Simon, and back to the scorebook. It went from feeling like a thin sheet of ice in my hands to feeling like a slab of hot steel. As I reached over to set it down, I had a hard time opening my fingers, a hard time letting go, even though I wanted nothing more than to get rid of it.

Simon jerked it away from me and slid it into his backpack. "That rumor about Kristin and Brett and the hotel room is true. What no one knows about is the next day." He pulled a tissue from the box on Coach's desk and blew his nose. "Kristin called me Sunday afternoon, thanked me for singing to her, asked me to meet her that evening. We met at Allan & Rosie's in Shawano so no one here would see us. She told me she was through with Brett, told me the song was the nicest thing a guy had ever done for her." He smirked, a look I'd never seen on his face before, and the lead-off slot from his Hanson/Delzer game flashed through my mind. Simon spoke: "And then she kissed me."

Holy shit, I thought, remembering how his lineup ended for that game. "You're not really going to…"

"Yes," he said, "I am. The top of the first doesn't end in that game for awhile." And as he said it, he smirked—the kind of smirk you see on someone's face when he knows, beyond a shadow of a doubt, that he is in control of a situation that he's going to wring until he squeezes out every last drop of what he wants from it.

My stomach gave a sudden twist, and I tasted something bitter in the back of my throat. "That's just wrong," I said.

"I know," Simon said, "but can you blame me?" He was still smirking.

Simon had me there—the abuse he'd taken went all the way back to elementary school, and looking back on it, it's a wonder he didn't turn into one of those kids who shows up at school with a gun and pipe bombs and makes the lead story on the nightly news. A mental snapshot of Simon rolled into a giant snowball during recess in second grade flashed through my mind.

"How about this?" he said, no longer smirking. "We only have a few games left this season. Feel like ending Senior year on a heroic note? Build on that grand slam off Watham?" Simon arched his eyebrows and went on. "You could show people feats of home run hitting like they've never seen before. Get your name in the school record books. You know," he said, "if I owned a major league team, I'd get as many power hitters as possible on the club. Chicks dig the long ball. It's sexy. It puts people in the seats, gets written up in the papers."

I remembered how unbelievably *good* it felt to make that kind of contact against Watham. And Simon was right about home runs—the players who were my heroes as I grew up were the big boppers, the players who could change the face of the game with a single swing of the bat. And though I was never one to hit for average, I could clear the fences when I did make contact. I was a half-dozen homers short of the school record. And though Simon may have sunk his claws into Kristin Hanson, Nicole Wolf had always seemed to give me a wider smile in first hour after I'd gone yard. I was planning on going to a private liberal arts school in the fall, planning on playing ball—maybe the coach could scrounge up an extra thousand in scholarship money for a slugger on the rise... And then I felt my stomach lurch again, tasted the bile in the back of my throat. *Shit*, I thought, and wished my parents hadn't made me go to church every Sunday since I could remember.

I thanked Simon for the offer but declined and began walking toward the door of Coach's office.

"You sure?" Simon asked.

I thought of Nicole in first hour and imagined her licking her pink-glossed lips. I reached for the door handle and shook my head. My stomach stopped churning.

"I just have to ask you one thing," Simon said. "You're not going to say anything—are you?" He placed his backpack in front of him on the desk and looked at me over the top of his glasses. His eyes narrowed and his lips pinched tightly together as he stared at me.

Good God, I thought. I pictured Brett writhing in the dirt. I again tasted something bitter in the back of my throat. "No," I said, "not a word." The doorknob was cool in my palm as I turned away from Simon and pushed open the door. "But I do have a question," I said and looked back. "A dozen games left in the scorebook—got any plans?"

The smirk came back to Simon's face. "You might say I've thought of a few things."

The Wide Turn Toward Home

Top of the Ninth

Jeff Luckow walked down the canned goods aisle at Owen's Fine Foods and ran his finger across the lip of the top shelf—right past the Mary Kitchen Hash and the generic sauerkraut—and pushed a mini-avalanche of dust to the scuffed tile floor. He bypassed the produce section, an aisle-end sale display of Maxwell House coffee and Nabisco snack crackers, and made his way to the meat case. He leaned over the steaks encased in bright pink styrofoam and taut plastic film and sniffed. Somewhere in the refrigerated chill of the fans, he detected a hint of decay, and when he inspected the steaks more closely, he could see the t-bones graying at their edges. Some things never change, he thought. He checked his watch. Almost 10 o'clock. He wasn't sure if the chill running through him came from the meat case or his anxiety.

Thirteen years earlier, Jeff had been a stock clerk at this grocery store, facing cans of creamed corn and making sure to keep the eggs near the top of the bags he packed. Thirteen years earlier he'd graduated from Gillett High School, packed his father's suitcase, and reported to rookie league ball in High Falls, Montana. He'd been back home to Wisconsin every off-season, helping his dad on the family dairy farm, performing the daily rituals of milking and feeding. In late October, they picked corn and plowed the fields for spring planting. Novembers, they hunted deer in the cedar swamps and hardwoods along the northern border of the Luckow family homestead. On the short days of December and January—before Jeff reported to Spring Training in Arizona—they went ice fishing through the thick ice of the lakes that dotted northern Oconto County.

The work, the hunting, the fishing were all familiar enough, but after Jeff had left that first summer—and after he received a phone call in the room he was renting above a garage in High Falls, Montana—Gillett never felt like home again. For the last thirteen years, "home" had been the ballpark. Boarding houses or apartments were places to sleep during the season, and the farm was a place to stay during the months leading up to Spring Training. Ballparks, though, always felt like home—their cramped locker rooms, dugouts littered with the husks of sunflower seeds, the bullpens open to the profane, beer-swilling fans. And the pitchers mound, even with runners taking their leads and a batter arching tobacco juice toward him, was home most of all.

He walked down the tissue and frozen goods aisle, hands jammed tightly into the pockets of a suit that made him itch every time he wore it, and went to the service counter. The Winston Cigarette calendar's digits had been flipped to read October 28. Jeff tapped his toe inside his cracked black wingtips and looked at the young woman standing behind the short plexi-glass window. "Any faxes yet, Annie?"

"Sorry, Mr. L—nothing yet." She continued sorting a stack of coupons, filing them in brown accordion folders.

"Wish I didn't have to bother you, but you're the only place in town with a fax machine." Jeff watched Annie slip the last of the coupons into a folder, then pull back her shoulders and stretch. Her navy blue smock couldn't hide the swell of her stomach. Annie caught him staring and cleared her throat. Jeff blushed and looked away. "Sorry," he said. "I…it's just…"

"Don't worry about it, Mr. L. No hiding it anymore," Annie said.

Jeff asked, "How far along?"

"Six months. Doctor says it'll be a Valentine's baby."

"You and…and the dad must be happy."

Annie placed the accordion folders beneath the counter. "I couldn't say how he feels, Mr. L. I haven't heard from him since the day after we graduated last June."

Jeff remembered how slippery it felt to hug someone in a graduation robe. "I'm sorry. I didn't know."

Annie almost laughed. "Don't worry about it. My folks are helping me out. Me and baby'll be okay." She began checking off items on a receiving slip.

Jeff kept watching the small fax machine on the desk behind Annie. He began talking to it in his mind. Come on, he thought, spit it out. He wanted the machine to beep and hiss and click, to see the contract Ray Daubach had promised him a day earlier. What he'd do with that promise once it had been delivered, he didn't know, but he at least wanted to see it—to hold it in his hands, to carefully read every word, to feel the weight it would (or wouldn't) create in his stomach. He wanted to be able to decide for himself which way to point the nose of his car when he left the parking lot of Owen's Fine Foods.

"Mr. L," Annie said, "you look like I felt whenever I had to give a speech in Ms. Smits' class."

Carolyn. There's no escape, is there? Jeff thought. He didn't know what to do with his hands. He loosened his tie. A cool rush of air raised goose bumps on his neck. He chuckled and looked down at his shoes. They needed to be shined.

Jeff stared into the electric eye above the sliding doors, turned around, and walked back to the freezer case. As he passed the Hungryman dinners, he mentally catalogued his high school classmates who were still living in Gillett. Almost without exception, Jeff knew the pattern of their lives. The guys got jobs making window frames at Linwood, made enough money to buy a souped-up 4 x 4 and get drunk on the weekends, then got into bar fights every few months to remind themselves they were still alive. The girls got pregnant and married, or didn't marry, these guys and worked in the canning factory or a store along Main Street. He kept walking, picking up cans, wondering if they'd come from Friday Canning just a few blocks up the street, and finally made his way back to the service desk. As he watched Annie, a question began forming, but he caught himself before asking it. Know when to leave well enough alone, he thought. He heard the labored click of the second hand climbing toward the twelve on the clock advertising Sun Drop soda. A picture of a much younger Carolyn flashed across his mind, followed by a picture of himself charging the pitcher's mound just a month earlier, ecstatic in a way he'd never been on a ball field. When he saw a woman with a baby in a child seat step into the checkout line, he couldn't hold back. "So, Annie—if you hadn't…if you didn't have a baby on the way, would you still be here?"

She looked at the counter and shook her head, then pushed away the receiving slip. She blew a quick puff of air through her nose—Jeff couldn't tell whether it was a snort or a chuckle—and said, "I wanted to go to college for music. To sing. You should've seen me in the school musical last April. We did *Bye Bye, Birdie.* I was Kim McAfee…I was accepted at Point, you know. You should hear me, Mr. L—I can really belt them out." She pulled her hair back into a ponytail and slipped a blue scrunchie around it.

Jeff watched Annie glancing at her stomach and tugging the bottom hem of her smock. "So this…means no more singing?" he asked. In his mind, he heard the shotgun report of a fastball exploding in a catcher's mitt, pictured the cocky smirk of J.R. Gold as he pulled at the polyester double-knit of his impossibly white jersey.

When Annie looked back up, her eyes flashed for a moment.

Then she shrugged her shoulders and asked, "Does church choir count?"

Jeff looked at the fax machine. Silent.

He shook his head. Why hold back now? he thought. "God knows you don't owe me an answer—but doesn't having this baby on the way make you feel like you've given up on something?"

Annie sighed, looked away from Jeff, and picked up a receiving slip from the counter.

"I'm sorry," Jeff said. "I didn't—"

"Certain things take priority, Mr. L." A cashier had come to the desk with a stack of dollar bills. Annie slid rolls of quarters in her direction. "But I don't think that means you ever really stop wanting—or dreaming."

Jeff's eyes met hers for a moment. He noted the color of Annie's eyes. Green. Like Carolyn's.

Annie spoke. "So now it's my turn, Mr. L—what about you? Did you ever picture moving back to Gillett after you were done playing ball, taking over Big Al's farm? Is that what you want?"

Jeff shoved his hands deeper into his pockets and scuffed the toe of his shoe over the floor. He thought of his dad, waiting for him at the bank. He thought of the fax that was supposed to arrive at any moment. He thought of Carolyn Smits.

Annie went on. "Ms. Smits was in here the other night. She couldn't stop talking about you when she came through the checkout."

Jeff sighed and wiped his brow; it left the back of his hand damp. He hadn't told her about the fax—hadn't told anyone—about how, after reading it, he just might get into his car, turn it away from the bank and a land contract, and make a long drive south on I-43. Jeff looked out the large plate-glass window onto Main Street. Deaf Dickie Miller pedaled by on his single-speed bike.

"You never answered my question, Mr. L—is that what you really want?"

First Inning

Even in the Arizona springtime, the rush of cool air felt good as Jeff stepped into Cactus Jack's Bar & Grill. Jeff saw him seated, alone, in a booth near the rear of the pub—Ray Daubach, Cream City's newly appointed executive vice president and general manager. He'd been Jeff's pitching coach at Single-A Beloit in '92. At least someone's managed to work his way up the ladder, Jeff thought.

The equipment manager had given him Daubach's note in the locker room after the game that earlier that afternoon. Jeff had just tossed a miserable inning and two-thirds (three runs on four hits and a pair of walks) against the Mariners' B-team in a split-squad contest. The last thing Jeff wanted to do was eat greasy food in a bad bar with the man who'd undoubtedly seen his performance. The man who was going to tell him that even this sorry organization no longer had room in its system for an over-the-hill pitcher whose arm had all the life of roadkill. As he stood just inside the door of the bar, Jeff contemplated turning around, walking out. Let 'em put a pink slip in my locker like anyone else, he thought. At least I can call myself a ballplayer for one more night. Daubach had spotted him, though, and motioned Jeff to join him.

As he approached the booth, Jeff watched Ray twist a wedge of lime into his beer and toss the pulpy triangle onto a stack of several others on the table. Before Jeff even sat, Daubach asked, "How's the wing?"

"Fine, just fine." Jeff slid into the booth.

"Bullshit. Looked limper than my grampa's dick this afternoon." He held up his index finger to the waitress, who brought over a pint of beer. "Here. This'll cure what ails you—goes down easy with a twist of lime. Make you forget all about the big bats those twenty year-olds were waving at you this afternoon."

Jeff knew that Ray's new role in the organization brought a whole new set of troubles, but the man sitting across the table from him was a far cry from the coach he'd known a decade earlier. "I'll take a rain check, boss."

"More for me," Ray said. He drank then ran his fingers through his thinning hair. "Maybe that's your problem. How much time you racked up in the Show these twelve years? A month?" He took a long pull from the glass meant for Jeff.

Jeff studied the wall behind Ray. It was painted to look like adobe—a hazy red in the half-light of the bar—complete with phony cracks and fake pockmarks. "Ray, I know what's coming. Just give it to me straight and I'll clear my locker."

Ray snorted. "Don't make an ass of yourself. Your gear's being moved to the minor league complex."

Jeff's stomach sank. "I figured on starting the season in Triple-A, but I was hoping that by June—or sooner, if someone got hurt—I'd get the call…" Moving to the minor league complex on the fringe of camp this early meant he'd be starting the season, at best, in Double-A ball. So much for this being the year, he thought.

Daubach put both hands flat on the table and leaned in toward Jeff. "Look, I may be king of the world for this bad excuse for a baseball team, but even this organization knows when to say when. You're thirty-one. Thirteenth season. Your arm's tank hit empty four years ago, doesn't even have vapors left—"

"I was only a game under .500 last season—ERA a hair over four—"

"And a damned impressive strikeout-to-walks ratio, too, right? Borderline acceptable if you're still twenty-five and can bring it ninety-plus. Triple A ain't the Show. Your fastball tops out at eighty-four, and I could probably pull a kid off a high school team who could match your numbers this spring."

Jeff's head felt as though it were floating, spinning three feet above the rest of his body. "Maybe I could learn the knuckler? Remember Niekro? Pitched 'til he was nearly fifty."

Ray laughed. "You're forgetting something, Jeff—I'm *not* cutting you loose, okay? I'm telling you that you don't have a snowball's chance of ever pitching in the Show—but I'm also telling you we want you." Ray grinned crookedly.

"So I can eat up innings in the Appalachian League? I don't think so." Jeff slid one leg out from beneath the table and began to get up from the booth.

"Hear me out." Ray pushed away his beer and looked at Jeff over the rim of the glass. Jeff took a deep breath and sat down, but he remained on the edge of the seat, ready to leave at any time. "We've got two decent starters in the rotation on the big club, Petersen and Myers; the other three couldn't piss into Lake Michigan if you stood them knee-deep in the water. What those two have, aside from youth and live arms, is smarts—they *know* how to *pitch*."

Jeff watched Ray pick a greasy tortilla chip out of the cloth-lined basket on the table and cram it into his mouth. Little pieces of the chip stuck to his lip as he chewed, then fell to the table. "And they have one other thing in common—Petersen was your roomie on road trips in Triple-A three years ago, Myers the season after that. I know you well enough to know you weren't out teaching them how to whore or swim in a pitcher of beer or shoot smack or toke the weed. Mr. Jeff Luckow's got 'em back at the hotel watching the late game from the coast on cable—talking some serious friggin' *baseball*, right?"

Jeff reached out and, in a single, sudden movement swept the bowl of tortillas from the table. A bouncer moved toward the booth, but Ray held up a hand, shook his head, and mouthed *it's okay*. "I don't get it," Jeff said. "I'm a good luck charm? Sit me on a stool in the clubhouse and let them all rub me before the game, is that it?" He leaned back. The bar's air conditioning had cooled the vinyl, and it felt good through his polo shirt.

Daubach laughed and motioned to the waitress for another beer. "Yeah, yeah—sit there in your jock like some Greek statue. Press catches wind, maybe we could change our name to the Fruits, eh? Nothing like a little notoriety." The waitress placed another beer on the table. Jeff watched Ray eye her as she walked toward the bar. "Mmm. Here's the deal, kid," Ray said. "The way I see it, you've got a hand in Myers and Petersen. The one thing you've always had is smarts. Saw it when I was your pitching coach in Beloit. That you've managed to hang on for as long as you have is proof of that—you've done more with less than any player I've ever seen. Joe Blow doesn't make it through a season in Single A with your arm."

Jeff felt his face turn red. He grabbed the napkin-wrapped silverware and shook loose the fork. He felt like stabbing the tines into the formica tabletop. "That how you climbed the ladder to the front office, stroking egos?"

"See? You've got smarts, kid—a ladder is just what I'm setting up for you." Ray sipped the head from his glass of beer.

"I don't follow."

"You're not going to be doing much pitching where you're going—just soak up innings in blowouts. You'll officially be a pitcher on the roster for High Desert; unofficially—more importantly—you're a big buddy for J.R. Gold." Daubach smiled as though he'd just dropped the golden goose into Jeff's lap.

"Where'd you get that brainstorm—been watching *Bull Durham*? What does me baby-sitting a prospect have to do with climbing the ladder?"

"Your shot in the Show's as a coach. Think of this as a test case, a dry run."

Jeff drummed his fingers on the table. He felt his ears growing hot. He wanted to stand up and tell Ray Daubach ugly things, maybe grab him by the neck and bring the bouncer over for real this time, but Jeff remained sitting. He stopped drumming his fingers, and looked up at the G.M. "So it's me and boy wonder, or I'm out?"

Ray chuckled, his breath escaping in short snorts. "Your words, not mine. You'll follow the kid—he goes to Double-A, you're there; Triple-A, you follow him. Get the picture? He's only eighteen, but we think he *could* be ready to be called up in September when the rosters expand—if you can shorten the learning curve. Kid's built like a brick shithouse hits triple digits on the gun. If you..." Daubach flicked a tiny tortilla crumb onto the floor. "We'll talk at the end of the season about your place in the organization."

Jeff stared at the ring Daubach's beer had left on the tabletop. He felt his stomach doing strange things. Over the last three seasons, the voice in the back of his head had told him that he'd never pitch in the Show—that the spirit was willing but the flesh was weak. He'd managed to shout down the voice as long as it was only his own, but now Ray's had echoed it—"*Limper than my grampa's dick...Your arm's tank hit empty four years ago, doesn't even have vapors left to go on*"—and Jeff felt like he should do something crazy for once in his life. He still felt like punching someone. A drunk tourist or Ray—feel the crunch of bone collapsing beneath his knuckles. Have a few drinks himself, find a fast car, and hit the desert highways, pushing the speedometer into triple digits. As soon as the thoughts flashed through his mind, though, Jeff knew he wouldn't. Knew he couldn't. He looked up at Ray. "Let me sleep on it?"

"Not a problem, kid. Admitting it's over is the hardest thing any player does. I kept at it a couple of years too long myself. Went on one hell of a bender when the Cards finally cut the cord." Ray finished his beer and set the glass down at the edge of the table. "But remember, kid—I'm giving you a shot. Hell, what are you going to do if you're not in baseball? Go back to damn Wisconsin and farm?"

Second Inning

Only a few dozen fans dotted the stands. Jeff was surprised to see even that many. Spring intrasquad games at the minor league camp seldom drew spectators. Today, though, had been the second outing of the spring for the phenom the baseball press had been buzzing about since

Cream City had selected him in the first round of the June free agent draft—Jeff's project, J.R. Gold, a year removed from high school. Another Texas fireballer—the next Ryan, the next Clemens, all the scouts said—throwing the kind of smoke that sent a catcher to the equipment man for extra padding in his mitt. Brick shithouse is about right, Jeff thought, remembering Ray's assessment of the pitcher as he ran with the Anointed One along the warning track. At 6' 8", J.R. Gold towered over Jeff, and his 240 pound girth cast an imposing shadow as they rounded the left-field corner. What I wouldn't give, Jeff thought. Freaking monster.

In his two inning stint, J.R. Gold had given the spectators plenty to talk about—five strikeouts, four walks, and a pair of wild pitches. The second wild pitch rocketed, on the fly, all the way to the backstop. The pitch had registered 101 mph on the Jugs gun, and Jeff had noticed J.R. smirking when the ball zipped into a seam between slabs of protective padding on the wall—admiring the wonder his arm had wrought while forgetting to cover the plate as a runner scored from third.

Jeff's legs felt heavy as they jogged toward the infield, his cleats rasping as they struck the red dirt. Jeff noticed that J.R. had barely broken a sweat, and that even at his size, the young pitcher moved easily, even gracefully, his strides a rhythmic counterpoint to the easy pumping of his arms. His cleats made no sound as they ran behind the plate, past the dugout on the first base side of the infield, then along the right field line and through the open fence in the outfield wall in right center.

Jeff took off his cap, tossed it to one side, and began his usual stretching routine. He sat on the grass, feeling the cool blades through his uniform pants. For a moment, the grass almost smelled like a freshly mown field of alfalfa, and he pictured his father pulling a haybine through the fields. Jeff extended both legs in front of him to form a V and reached toward his right foot. Feeling tightness in his hamstring, Jeff bent forward slowly, careful not to push tendons past the point of mild protest.

"Sucks to be old," said J.R., leaning against the fence, chuckling. He looked up as a military jet roared overhead, a training flight from the Air Force base twenty miles away.

Jeff had grown accustomed to J.R.'s comments about his age. "You'll know it soon enough if you don't stretch out and go to the trainer for treatment on your arm." Jeff pulled his feet close with his knees in the air and leaned forward between them.

"Damn, that jet's got speed." J.R. reached back to grab his raised foot and did a half-hearted quad stretch. "Speed's why they can have their way with the bad guys—they don't even know what hit 'em. Some freakin' Arab's in his bunker babbling 'Allah, Allah, Allah' and *wham*! F-16 turns him into a crispy critter before he knows it."

"So now you're the Secretary of Defense?" Jeff shook his head as he sat in the butterfly position. His groin wasn't enjoying it.

"Ya'll never know," J.R. said. "I'm like that jet, you know— we've both got afterburners. Very useful when it comes to deliverin' payload. Maybe that'll be my nickname, eh? Jet? Call my fastball 'Cruise,' like the missile?"

"You ought to be worrying about covering the plate on wild pitches before you worry about nicknames, 'Jet.'" Jeff stood and began a set of torso rotations. He felt his lower back protest. Damn. "What were you thinking about when that runner scored?"

J.R. laughed. "Did you see the way that ball lodged into the padding? That took some serious smoke, old man."

"It wouldn't have sailed on you if you hadn't dropped down to the side—you're better off coming in from over the top. And you didn't answer my question—what were you thinking?"

J.R. smirked, scratched his chest, and pulled at his jersey. "It's only Spring Training, man—my head'll be there when I'm firing live ammo. Don't worry about it."

Jeff stopped his rotations. "But I am, wonderboy."

J.R. smirked. "I know I should appreciate you taking a shine to me. Who needs an iPod with your yappin' in the background these last couple of weeks? But honestly, if you've got so much goin' on, what're you doin' down here in the boonies? When I was a kid, I never saw you on ESPN. How long have you been at this business? Seven, eight years? I know I'm just putting in time here. It's like my agent said, 'They didn't give you a $5 million bonus to bounce around the bushes, son.'"

Jeff looked to the parking lot sandwiched between the minor league complex and the parent club's training facility. "Actually, it's been twelve years," he said in a low voice. A Corvette snarled before screeching out the lot from the section reserved for the players in the major league camp. Jeff picked up his glove from the grass. "You may not be bouncing for long, Mr. Gold, but you can bounce a lot less if you clean the cotton out of your ears and start exercising the muscle inside your cranium." He spit in the direction of the parking lot. "So what did your agent figure was a reasonable stretch in the boonies before you assume your throne?"

J.R.'s eyes narrowed. He stood with all of his weight on his left foot and crossed his arms over his chest. "Two years—three years tops…must be hard for you to comprehend, eh?" He chuckled.

Jeff thought of his own month in the Show. "Well let me share a little secret with you—your agent doesn't know squat."

"I'm not you, old man. This wing's gonna take me places." J.R. watched the parent club's left fielder get into an Escalade. "That's gonna be me…have some swimsuit model in the passenger seat…gonna be sweet."

"So the girl from back home doesn't come with you when you hit the big time?" Jeff asked, referring to the senior picture that had fallen out of J.R.'s wallet as they dressed in the clubhouse earlier in the week— a shot of a cute blonde with typically Texan big hair. "Oh, I don't doubt that your arm's going to take you there. It's just that it can get you there yet this season." Jeff saw J.R.'s eyes lock on his for the first time since they'd finished their run. "You like the sound of that, hmm?"

"Just the first thing you've said all day worth listening to, old man."

Jeff laughed. "Your thinking I've 'taken a shine' to you shows how much some people love themselves." He mentally weighed what he was about to say, considered the pros and cons. Well, 'coach,' Jeff thought, you always appreciated the straight scoop, the no bullshit approach. He decided to continue. "If that arm of yours weren't my meal ticket, too, we wouldn't be having this conversation."

J.R. cocked his head and looked at Jeff skeptically. "I don't follow."

"My yappin' is my trying to screw your head on straight and teach you a few things about pitching other than chucking for all you're worth until you blow out your shoulder or elbow and lose two seasons to rehab and ten miles an hour off your fastball." Jeff gave J.R. the abbreviated version of his conversation with Ray Daubach two weeks earlier. He tried to remain firm and matter-of-fact, but he hated what he was doing. He hated that his own arm couldn't do what came so naturally to J.R. Gold, hated that the kid's brain operated as reluctantly as the machinery on Big Al's farm on a frigid January morning. He saw, though, the story slowly sinking in as a smile spread across J.R.'s face. "I'm not trying to be your buddy, 'Golden Boy'—your signing bonus has bought you enough of those I'm sure—but we both want to get to the same place. Isn't that enough?"

J.R. arched his eyebrow. "This season?"

"This season."

"And I just have to do what you say?"

"If you want Heidi Klum instead of 'Miss Texas Rodeo Queen' riding shotgun any time soon."

"They always say those who can't, teach." J.R. snickered. "Twelve seasons, eh?"

"Thanks for the resounding vote of confidence, Mr. Gold— internalize what I tell you as well as you stroke egos, there's no telling what you may do." Jeff saw Daubach in the parking lot, walking toward his Mercedes-Benz, and bent over to pick up his cap. The grass still smelled like alfalfa. "Get ice on that arm, kid."

Third Inning

Lyle Lovett's understated twang floated from the speakers of Jeff's '93 Corolla as he pulled into a narrow slot in the parking garage of Phoenix International Airport. Jeff sang along in the slightly off-key baritone he reserved for those moments he was alone in the car—"That's right, you're not from Texas…but Texas wants you anyway…" Jeff had many reasons to feel good—J.R. had thrown three shutout innings earlier in the day, walking only one and keeping his delivery straight over the top (but we need to talk about pitch location tomorrow, Jeff thought). Jeff had pitched also, working his way out of a bases-loaded jam in the seventh by pulling the string on a change-up that made the batter look foolish (who cares if he's a nineteen year-old who'll probably never see a major league roster, Jeff thought)—he loved putting the perfect pitch in the perfect spot in a crucial situation. It was a beautiful thing, a feat that made Jeff feel as though he were floating back to the dugout. And he was about to pick up his father, down from Wisconsin for his annual Spring Training visit.

Jeff's father, "Big Al" to the locals back in Gillett, enjoyed catching a week's worth of Arizona sun and exhibition games before going back to Wisconsin to begin preparations for spring planting. Jeff thought the warm weather would really do him well this year. That winter, his father had finally acknowledged the accumulated effects thirty years of dairy farming had taken on his body. Advil, glucosimine, and chondroitin had become an additional course at each of his meals, the heating pad had taken a permanent spot draped over the arm of his La-Z-Boy, and the strong smell of liniment followed him everywhere. When they'd last spoken, Big Al told him that he'd be watching games from the third base side this year (as opposed to his customary perch somewhere behind the plate, the best view for watching Jeff work), so as to stay in the sunshine for the entire contest. "Good for aching knees," he said.

Big Al had never complained about any physical problems, so to hear him even mention it over the phone had caught Jeff off-guard—but not as much as Big Al's mention of a surprise he wanted to share with him in Arizona. "A couple of them, actually…not something I want to go into at just this moment," he said, "but we definitely have some things to talk about down there." Surprises were as foreign to his father as snowstorms in July—Jeff couldn't remember a Christmas or birthday from his youth when, courtesy of Big Al, he hadn't known almost every one of his presents at least a month early, a fact that had annoyed his mother to no end.

Jeff checked his watch as he walked through the sliding doors of the terminal. 7:15. His father's plane was due to arrive at 7:52, so Jeff found the newsstand tucked neatly between the airport lounge and a Burger King, pulled a copy of *The Sporting News Baseball Annual* off the magazine rack, and went to the cash register. He flipped through the glossy pages as he stood in line behind a woman with a baby in a stroller. She shuffled through her purse, talking to herself under her breath. Her son looked at Jeff and laughed a baby laugh like a high-pitched hiccup. The child's green eyes danced, and a string of clear saliva trickled down from the corner of his mouth and dangled from his round, fleshy chin, gradually lengthening until it dotted the "i" in "Li'l Slugger" printed across the front of his terry cloth outfit. Jeff chuckled and, without thinking, stuck his tongue out at the baby. The baby raised his wisps of red eyebrows, burped so loudly Jeff could feel it, then gurgled and smiled back.

When the woman heard her son burp, she pulled her hand from her purse and said, "Alex!" Her compact clattered to the floor and skidded toward Jeff, stopping just short of his loafers. Jeff and the woman both bent to pick it up at the same time, but Jeff beat her to it. From his knees, he handed the compact to the woman. For a moment, he felt as if he were caught in a scene from a B-movie, one where two former lovers who haven't seen each other for years meet by blindest chance.

When he made eye contact with her, a name he hadn't thought about in quite some time flashed through his mind. The green eyes, the loose, red-brown curls, the hint of freckles across the bridge of her nose. The chin wasn't the same, though—a bit narrower perhaps, and her neck a bit shorter. "Thanks," the woman said.

Jeff couldn't respond for a moment. "Not a problem." They both stood. The baby had his arms straight out, his tiny fingers grasping air as he blew spittle out through his pursed, burbling lips.

The woman put her compact back into her purse, pulled out a five dollar bill, and paid for the copy of *Entertainment Weekly* on the counter by the cash register. "Okay, Alex," she said and slipped her purse over her shoulder and grabbed the curved handles of the stroller. "We've got a plane to catch, little man." She ran her fingers through her son's red hair, then said to Jeff, "Thanks again."

"You bet." Even her voice, he thought. Jeff shook his head. It had been a long time since he'd thought of Carolyn, longer still since he'd seen her. She didn't even come back to Gillett for the holidays anymore—hadn't since she'd married someone she'd met her sophomore year of college. Jeff paid for his magazine, left the newsstand, and looked across the airport concourse for the woman and her child. They'd vanished.

Jeff walked to the gate where his father was to arrive and sat down to wait. The vinyl of the chair squeaked as he settled in and flipped to the section giving one baseball scribe's forecast for Cream City. He had a hard time focusing as he tried to read the article. As he scanned the section examining the team's pitching prospects (no "Jeff Luckow" mentioned in boldface italics), he pictured another airport scene, this one from June of 1989—he'd looked back from the tunnel leading to the plane that would carry him to his Rookie League assignment and saw Carolyn, standing by the United ticket counter. She wore a flowered sundress, and she had wrapped her bare arms, tanned a light brown, around her stomach, holding herself in the chill of the air conditioning.

But it was her look, or more properly the lack of one, that had stayed with Jeff. It stayed with him all through that summer as he tried to tell himself that maybe, *maybe*, things would work themselves out, go back to the way they'd been when they plotted their future in the months before graduation. They would leave Gillett—Carolyn would go to the Twin Cities, study English, and become a high school teacher wherever Jeff found a home on a major league roster after working his way up

94

through the minors—and they'd promised they would always *be*, a fact of nature.

When Carolyn called Jeff in Montana two days later, her voice was cold and metallic over the long-distance connection. She was calling from a pay phone outside a clinic in Cream City. "I've taken care..." Jeff heard her swallow in the silence. "I've taken care of everything," she said. Jeff pictured her in the airport, and it suddenly became impossibly concrete, impossibly real, so impossibly *heavy* as it traveled from his mind's eye to the pit of his stomach. She hadn't taken care of anything, really. The weight of what they shared with no one else changed everything. When Jeff and Carolyn next saw each other, in the lobby of her dormitory that fall, they kissed and held each other, but the gestures of tenderness seemed almost obligatory. They spent the weekend together, but nothing felt the same—the easy laughter was gone, and their conversations were forced, chatter about everything other than what they wanted to discuss.

Jeff quit trying to read the magazine and instead watched people walk past. An Asian man was carrying ski poles. An elderly woman had stopped in the middle of the concourse, using one hand to keep her balance against her walker while she used the thumb of her other hand to adjust her dentures. And a young man in an Arizona State sweatshirt and a red Santa Claus hat glided past. You're a bit late, Jeff thought. He remembered how, when Carolyn had come home for Christmas that first year after high school, they met to exchange gifts. The heavy feeling had come back to Jeff's stomach as they sat in her family's living room. The white lights on the Christmas tree twinkled in the dim light of the afternoon. He could feel it—this would be the last time they would ever exchange gifts.

Carolyn's present to Jeff was wrapped in a rich burgundy paper accented by a gold foil bow. He carefully removed the bow and pulled the paper away from the box. Inside, swaddled in white tissue paper, was a woodcarving—a hand, its wrist the base, gripping a baseball, stained a rich cherry red and burnished to a satiny finish. "A curveball grip...my pitch," he said. Jeff handed Carolyn a narrow box. She opened it and removed a bracelet—a thin gold chain with a string of a dozen freshwater pearls. The pearls were small and far from perfect, but Jeff had chosen the bracelet for sentimental reasons.

A young couple passed Jeff in the terminal. Each of them wore a backpack and hiking boots. Jeff wondered if they might be heading to

95

camp on the lip of the Grand Canyon—and remembered the camping trip the summer before his senior year, the trip when he and Carolyn started dating. With a group of friends, they'd taken a road trip to the Dells and camped along the Wisconsin River. On the night of August 12, the third night of the trip, Jeff and Carolyn had slipped away from the others and went for a swim. Jeff had been flirting with Carolyn ever since they'd started down Highway 47 in Aaron Kline's rusted '78 Jeep Wagoneer, and his suspicion that she enjoyed his best efforts at witty repartee were confirmed by the way she flipped back her hair, flashed him a smile, and said "Catch me if you can" when he suggested they check out the water temperature. The half-moon provided more than enough light to give the ripples on the water's surface a fish scale effect. The water was warm, and the current was gentle. Carolyn was the better swimmer of the two, and to Jeff's frustration, she kept herself just out of his reach as he swam after her out in the middle of the wide channel, only occasionally allowing him to *just* touch her—a quick brush of the palm of his hand over her denim cut-offs, the graze of his fingertips across the sole of her foot. "You're lucky I'm not really trying," Jeff said, pretending not to be interested.

"Why's that?" Carolyn replied, short of breath, her laughter rolling over the surface of the river. She stopped swimming and began treading, the silver water rolling off her arms.

"Because you'd really be in for it," Jeff said, now treading water himself, just out of arm's reach of Carolyn.

"Some people are just all talk and no—"

Jeff didn't give her a chance to finish her sentence. He scissor-kicked toward Carolyn and kissed her. In his haste (and in fifteen feet of water), though, his aim wasn't true, and he'd wound up knocking his front teeth against the point of her chin. Carolyn laughed. "Is that how you try to impress all the girls?"

Jeff was glad that she couldn't see him blushing in the half-light. Smooth move, Ex-Lax, he thought. His mind raced for a snappy come-back. "Not usually…I save that one for the ones with 'toothsome' smiles."

"Mrs. Lucht would be so proud of your vocabulary—I suppose you deserve another chance."

Carolyn motioned for Jeff to follow her into the shallow water. They knelt in the soft silt a few feet from shore and kissed, much more successfully this time. Jeff couldn't be sure of how much time had passed before he felt Carolyn abruptly pull away and shout, "Ouch!"

"Oh my god, I'm so sorry—I—"

Carolyn laughed. "No, no, no—trust me, you're fine." She took her hand from Jeff's arm and reached down into the silt, near her knee. She pulled out a clam. "Must've been this."

Jeff held out his hand and Carolyn gave him the clam. Its shell was deeply ridged and almost perfectly symmetrical. The clam fit precisely in the palm of Jeff's hand. He held it up and looked at it more carefully. Its halves were just parted, and the top shell had a jagged edge. "Killer clam eats swimmer's knee—I can just see the headlines back home in the *Times-Herald*."

"Very funny," Carolyn said. She placed her fingertips against Jeff's chest and gently pushed him. "Let me have a closer look." She took the clam from Jeff. Using her thumbs, she opened the clam a bit further and looked in. "Anybody home?" She paused a beat. "Must be out for the evening."

"Here, let me see." Jeff opened the clam completely and held it so that the light of the half moon fell fully into the parted shells. He and Carolyn both peered inside. There, in the bottom half, the moonlight outlined a small object, something roughly oval, perhaps a half-inch long. Jeff picked it out and held it in the palm of his hand. He could just make out cloudy swirls, and though its surface was irregular, it was made of a smooth, hard substance with an almost milky texture. "What is it?" he asked.

"I think it's a pearl," Carolyn said. "My grandmother has a bracelet of freshwater pearls, and this looks an awful lot like one of those."

"In that case—" Jeff closed his fingers around the pearl and stood up, helping Carolyn to her feet as well. He gave her an exaggerated bow, then sank to one knee and asked her to hold out her hand. "For you, m'lady," he said, placing the pearl in her hand.

Carolyn laughed and, lifting one foot high out of the water, began jogging to the riverbank. "You're such a dork..." she said, her voice teasing. She sat on a fallen tree along the bank and smiled at Jeff. He swore that he saw her green eyes dancing in the moonlight. "...But that's what makes you so cute."

"Now arriving at Gate D, American Flight 783 ...Flight 783 at Gate D." The disembodied voice was cold, metallic. Jeff looked at his ruined magazine; he hadn't realized that he'd been rolling and unrolling the magazine, twisting it over and over to keep his hands busy as his mind wandered. He peeled his forearm from the chair and checked his watch. 7:52. His father was right on time.

When his father exited the tunnel, Jeff immediately noticed the limp. An occasional hobble wasn't unusual for Big Al—seemed to hit him every time a front came through over the last few years—but this limp was more noticeable than any Jeff had seen from his father before. "Hey there. Let me get that for you." Jeff took his carry-on, an over-sized Buick tote bag the dealer had given him when he bought the Le Sabre two years ago. Jeff noticed a copy of *The Sporting News Baseball Annual* peeking out from the bag's exterior pocket. "What happened to you—some careless airport employee run over your foot with his electric cart?"

Big Al snorted. "Don't I wish. Cow nailed me a good one a week ago. Bruised all the way from my hip to my knee."

"You're lucky it wasn't worse." Jeff led him away from the gate and they walked toward the baggage claim.

"Thought it was at first." Big Al's right foot skimmed the floor tiles as they walked, and Jeff could tell that he avoided putting weight on his injured leg. "I must be a tough son of a gun."

Jeff knew that was an understatement—over the course of his career, he'd have liked to give several teammates just a fraction of Big Al's toughness. "Don't flatter yourself, old guy," he said, winking at his father.

"But if I don't, who will?" As they waited for Big Al's luggage to come up the ramp to the carousel, Big Al asked about Jeff's prospects for the season. The way he asked caught Jeff off-guard; he'd become rather businesslike, almost formal—a far cry from the boyishness that typically came over him whenever they talked baseball.

Jeff told him about his re-assignment to the minor league camp, but thinking of that strikeout earlier in the day, the ballplayer in Jeff wouldn't let him mention his training J.R. Gold or Ray Daubach's carrot on the stick. He still believed that, given a shot, he could make it.

His father responded with a simple, "Oh" and turned away. Jeff thought he'd seen him smile just a bit, and he knew he'd also heard Big Al let out a "hmmph." "There's my bag." Jeff recognized the battered yellow leather American Tourister suitcase and pulled it off the carousel—the same suitcase his father had insisted he use when he reported to Great Falls in the summer of 1989. It wasn't heavy. Jeff knew Big Al had probably packed one pair of pants (he guessed gray polyester) and maybe three plaid short-sleeve shirts (like the one he was wearing) that passed for chic among the retirement crowd that swarmed Phoenix that time of year. "Let me take it," Big Al said. "I'm not completely washed up."

"Worry about dragging around that leg of yours for now; I can handle this suitcase." They made their way through the terminal and out to the parking garage, tossed Big Al's bags into the trunk of the Corolla, and drove onto the beltway, heading for the Motel 6 where his father always stayed. Jeff waited for his father to bring up the surprises he'd mentioned over the phone, but their conversation in the car dealt with relatively superficial matters. Big Al complained that Phoenix needed a good polka station as Lyle Lovett and Randy Newman's cover of "Long, Tall Texan" came through the speakers. Jeff inquired about Jody, the hired man Big Al had kept working for him since Jeff's mother had died in June of '95. They both complained that George Steinbrenner had too damn much money to spend on the Yankees--"Nothing but buying the Series, if you ask me," Big Al said at least three times. After they arrived at the hotel and Big Al checked in, Jeff carried his father's suitcase to his room. "This joint looks as seedy as ever—you really ought to spring for a nicer place one of these years, maybe Holiday Inn or the Radisson."

"Works for me as long as I don't have cockroaches crawling under the covers with me," Big Al said. He rubbed his hip and then let his thick fingers move to his stomach. "I could go for some dinner— didn't even try eating that airplane food—feel like joining me? Old man's treat. Maybe that place we found last year…"

Great, Jeff thought. An image of Ray Daubach spraying pieces of tortilla chips flashed through Jeff's mind. But I suppose that dive would pass for five-star cuisine back home. "Cactus Jack's? You sure about that? I think you just liked the look of that blonde waitress working there last year."

Big Al grinned. "I was just thinking about how they serve up a mean plate of nachos, but now that you mention it, she was easy on the eyes, wasn't she?" Big Al yawned, then rubbed his index finger along the edge of his nose. "Besides," he said, "surprises are better on a full stomach."

Jeff didn't feel like eating. His father had never been so hard to pin down, and Big Al's refusal to show his cards took away whatever

99

buzz had been left over from earlier in the day. They both ordered Cokes; Jeff let his sweat a ring on the table. He'd ordered a seafood chimichanga that he watched go cold on the plate. Big Al made short work of a large platter of nachos heaped with seasoned ground beef, refried beans, and sour cream doused in liquid cheese such a bright orange it almost hurt Jeff's eyes. He tried to force Big Al's hand as he ate, but his father wouldn't be prodded. "I'm learning patience in my old age," he said. "Just think of this as making up for all the surprises I ruined for you when you were a kid." After he ate the last soggy nacho, Big Al ordered a beer, then twisted his face when he drank. "Think I'd learn—stuff tastes like pee water down here. We're not in Wisconsin any more."

Jeff poked at the chimichanga, surveyed the wreckage on Big Al's nacho platter, and sized up his father. "Okay," he said, "your belly's full, so can we be out with whatever it is?"

Big Al ran the thumb of his right hand over the callused palm of his left hand, drew a deep breath, and looked at Jeff. "Good news or bad news first?"

"It doesn't matter."

"Okay—surprise number one: I'm retiring."

Jeff was surprised—he sat up straight, pulled in his chin, and raised his eyebrows. He'd been expecting his father to tell him that he was going to marry one of the many available older women with whom he was so popular since Jeff's mother had died. He'd never pictured his father giving up farming. Jeff knew that Big Al loved the land as much as he loved baseball, and loved that it had been Luckow land since the family had come to Wisconsin from Germany in 1895.

"Well, semi-retiring may be more accurate. When I went in to see the doctor after that cow kicked me, he took some x-rays. Told me I don't have a speck of cartilage left in my knees or hips. It's just not as easy toughing it out anymore. Doctor said I need new knees and new hips, but there's no way he'd put them in as long as I was still farming. Driving tractor would be okay, but if I kept milking, those joints wouldn't last long with all the bending and crouching."

Oh shit, Jeff thought.

"Yep," said Big Al, "it'll be a big change for sure." He went on, talking about some of the particulars of joint replacement—cost, recovery time, the number of operations he'd need, the things he could and couldn't do with titanium joints—but Jeff only half-listened. He'd subdued the voice screaming in his head and forced himself to focus on another question: what would become of the farm his great-grandfather had homesteaded, the land his father loved? The hired man Jody was a hard worker—he took directions well, was good with the cows, and was talented mechanically, but he'd been in the learning disability program at school and had dropped out after his sophomore year; Jeff doubted he could handle the business end of the operation. And Jeff knew his father would never sell out to one of the corporate mega-farms; more than once he'd said hell would freeze over before they got their hands on Luckow land. Jeff had no siblings. The screaming voice came back.

"Dad," Jeff said, "you're not going to…"

His father was no longer looking down at the table or his hands. "I know what you're thinking—don't think I haven't been up lots of nights. God knows I've stood behind you as much as anyone has." His jawline was square, solid, and he spoke in a low, earnest tone. "Jeff, this is your thirteenth season. You've been shipped to the minor league complex for assignment…and when a player hasn't made it by the time he hits thirty, it's over." His father paused.

Jeff kept his head down but knew that his father was eyeing him carefully—his clenched jaw, his fingers drumming the table. Big Al continued. "The land has been good to me, good to this family. I can't let it go anywhere else, let it go *to* anyone else. It's not an easy life, but the land—I *know* this—the land will be good to you."

Jeff understood where his father was coming from. He understood, in a sense, the truth and inevitability of what he said, but he couldn't accept it. He pictured J.R. Gold on the mound earlier in the day, his motion fluid as he effortlessly exploded toward the plate. He heard the shotgun blast of J.R.'s fastball hitting the catcher's mitt and the umpire's "Aaaiiiiiiirggghhk" strike call.

Big Al continued. "I know you need to end things on *your* terms—I understand that." He scratched the side of his head, his fingers working through the gray hair that grew in loose waves from his temple. "I want you to play one last season—make peace with the game, make peace with yourself…you've earned the right to do that. I can make a go of it for another six months." He pushed his empty nacho platter to the edge of the table. "Right now, I don't want a yes or no. I just dropped one helluva surprise on you. Take some time to think about it, but in the end, I think you'll agree with me." Big Al paused and looked to something only he could see hovering in the dim light of the restaurant. "You know, your mom and I didn't come right back to the farm after my tour in Vietnam was over. We thought that once we'd left Gillett, we'd never go back." He raised his glass and sipped his beer. "Piss water…if nothing else, the beer's better up there."

The ballplayer in Jeff was cursing Big Al, drawing battle lines and declaring he'd never go back. Another part of Jeff pictured the pitcher's mound Big Al had built for him between the lilac bushes east of the farmhouse, remembered the scent a sea of soft purple blossoms produced as he taught himself the curveball on a warm Sunday in May after reading an interview with Sal Maglie he'd found in the school library. And then he remembered how, two years after that Sunday, he'd picked bunches of blossoms from those bushes, placed them in water in a blue glass vase, and had taken them to Carolyn as he went to pick her up before their graduation ceremony. She had cried when she said "They're so beautiful" and set them on her family's kitchen table, bending slightly to place her nose just above them and deeply breathe in their fragrance.

Jeff looked at his father now. He couldn't speak for several seconds. "I thought you said you had two surprises."

"I do—just thought you might want some time before I told you this one."

"You might as well fire the second barrel."

Big Al paused. Jeff noticed him looking in the direction of the bar where an attractive blonde was drawing a beer from the tap. Big Al placed both hands flat on the table and looked back to Jeff. "Carolyn Smits just moved back to Gillett."

Fourth Inning

Jeff made the slow stroll to the mound, where J.R. Gold angrily kicked at the dirt in front of the rubber, his cleats sending a fine spray of soil down the slope of the low hill, and the catcher, Simmons, talked to the pitcher from behind his mitt. On the orders of Ray Daubach, High Desert's manager had made Jeff the point man when J.R. needed a visit on the mound. Jeff walked with a practiced stride intended to give the relief pitcher warming up in the bullpen time to get in another pitch or two. It was the bottom of the seventh, two down, runners on second and third—the result of a walk on four pitches and a poorly placed fastball. Rancho Cucamonga's number three hitter had slapped down the foul line past the third baseman for a double. High Desert led 2-0.

Jeff could tell that J.R. Gold wasn't happy to see his approach—he'd stopped kicking the dirt and now stood with his hands on his hips, glaring at Jeff. Great, Jeff thought, it's happy fun time at the asylum.

He didn't bother addressing J.R.—Jeff knew he'd hear plenty from him anyway—and instead asked Simmons, "How much is left in the tank?"

Simmons replied, "He seems to—"

J.R. interrupted. "Tank's plenty full."

"I didn't ask you," Jeff said.

"Three-quarters of a tank of high octane," J.R. said. "Haven't even kicked in the turbo-chargers yet." J.R. took off his glove and began wringing the ball, twisting it deliberately with his long fingers.

Jeff shoved his hands deep into the pocket of his warm-up jacket and spit toward home plate without taking his eyes off J.R. "I asked Simmons. How much in the tank, Simmons?"

"About time for a re-fill," Simmons said.

"The hell it is," J.R. said. "Needle's nowhere near E. I'm good to go. The next guy's mine."

Jeff noticed that J.R. had sweat through his cap even though the springtime evening air was crisp in the high altitude of their home park, noticed that he breathed heavily, his chest visibly rising and falling beneath the loose polyester of his uniform. Jeff looked to the bullpen, where North was throwing in earnest. The last time North had come into a game with runners on base, he'd let his nerves get the best of him and walked the first three hitters he faced on twelve pitches. From the looks of J.R.—and from the way he'd grooved the last pitch—Jeff knew that he was, if not completely so, as close to finished for the night as he could get. Gut check first, he thought. "Then what happened on that last pitch?"

"Bastard got lucky," J.R. said.

Gut's okay, Jeff thought, so how about the head? "Simmons, what was the pitch the lucky bastard hit for a double?"

"Fastball, out over the plate," he said.

"How many fastballs in a row did Mario Andretti here throw the lucky bastard?"

"That was the fifth one."

"Fifth one." Jeff shook his head slowly and looked at J.R. "You shook off the sign on the last three pitches."

"I told you, he got lucky—couldn't touch my fastball first two

103

ups." J.R. took off his cap and wiped the sleeve of his undershirt across his forehead.

When he saw the umpire start for the mound to end the meeting, Jeff knew he had to wrap things up. "Even lucky bastards can catch up with the heat when it's the only thing they see. Trust your change-up. Throw the curve. Change locations. Andretti doesn't keep it in the same gear for the entire race."

The umpire reached the mound. "Okay, boys—time to break up the party."

"Gotcha, blue," Jeff said without looking at the umpire. He let J.R. keep the ball and stepped closer to him, his eyes inches away from the pitcher's chin, but through force of will made J.R. look down at him and make eye contact. He was still breathing heavily. Whew, he thought, bugger's got bad breath. Jeff searched his eyes. Yeah…he's got enough for one more. "Look at me, Mario. Whatever happens, this is your last hitter. Use your head. Make it count. And for Christ's sake, brush your teeth, kid."

Jeff watched from the dugout as J.R. made his pitches count, working Rancho Cucamonga's clean-up hitter from the inside out, striking him out on four pitches, the last of them a change-up that seemed to crawl to the plate by comparison to his fastball. The hitter practically screwed himself into the ground swinging at it. When J.R. came back to the dugout, Jeff waved him into the empty seat next to him along the bench. Teacher time, Jeff thought. "What was that you used to strike him out?"

"Change," J.R. said, pulling on his warm-up jacket.

"Where'd you spot the pitch before the strike out?"

"In on the hands." J.R. pulled a packet of sunflower seeds from the pocket of the jacket and poured several into his hand. He popped them into his mouth and began chewing.

"Where was the change-up?"

In rapid succession, J.R. spit the husks of sunflower seeds onto the dugout steps. "Low and away."

Jeff watched Rancho Cucamonga's pitcher warming up on the mound. Jeff had always appreciated coaches who didn't try to do too much at once, who had a goal in mind, worked toward it without browbeating, and then left well enough alone. Without looking at J.R., he asked, "Point made?"

"Affirmative, gramps."

"That's *Mister* gramps to you, Mario." Out the corner of his eye, Jeff saw J.R. roll his eyes before shaking his head and smiling.

It wasn't the first time Jeff had heard J.R. give the affirmative to a lesson he was trying to drive home. He hoped that this time it really stuck. Daubach had been right about J.R.'s stuff—Jeff had never seen a hurler in his thirteen years whose pitches were as electric as those thrown by J.R. And he made it look so damn easy. J.R.'s motion was effortless, and his mechanics were perfect. When he'd talked with Daubach about the J.R. prior to meeting him, Jeff's primary concern had been mechanics—he'd seen too many young pitchers shred rotator cuffs or pop elbow ligaments because they didn't realize the work that the legs and torso performed in optimally pitching a baseball. But after seeing him throw, he knew that J.R. did naturally what many of the best of pitchers had to labor over for years. Physically, J.R. had been built to pitch—a fact Jeff simultaneously held in awe and loathed. The part of him that refused to let go of the dream of pitching in the Show was jealous, jealous that an eighteen year-old from Texas who seemed to have marshmallows for brains. "You could top an ice cream sundae with 'em," High Desert's manager, Phil "Scrap Metal" Bowie had told Jeff after his first conversation with the Anointed One. J.R.'s demeanor was equal doses Ross Perot, Dubya, and skater punk.

That demeanor and those marshmallow brains were what concerned Jeff. Off the field, it wasn't an issue. Over the course of his career, Jeff had run into his share of flakes—like the second baseman signed out of the Mexican League who kept a sealed Igloo cooler full of pulque in the trunk of a rusted Chevy Nova. The relief pitcher who ate the insects he found underneath the bench in the bullpen. The catcher who washed his hands between innings and changed sanitary socks four times a game because "cleanliness is next to godliness." J.R.'s eccentricities were mild by comparison. He'd single-handedly driven up the price of stocks in the beverage company that produced Yoohoo chocolate drink, and he kept a photo of his high school sweetheart— Kristin Russell— tucked into the sweatband of his cap. And Jeff had to admit that most ballplayers didn't need to be Rhodes Scholars; so long as they could cross the street without being hit by a car, put their jocks on cup to the front, and kept their shoes tied, they were good to go once they took the field.

Pitchers, though, were a different story, and Jeff knew he'd have to get J.R. to think on the mound—no matter how much heat his fastball brought or how sharply his curveball broke, Jeff knew J.R. would have to stay one step ahead of hitters as he climbed the ladder. He would have to be able to spot his pitches, would have to avoid his impulsiveness and his headstrong tendency to try overpowering hitters with a fastball over the heart of the plate in tight spots.

Both teams went down in order in the eighth. North was surprisingly calm as he induced the first two Rancho Cucamonga hitters to ground out, then retired the final hitter on fly ball that nearly reached the warning track. Jeff would have liked to point out to J.R. that the ground outs came about because North had kept the ball down in the strike zone and that the fly out should have left the park (North had hung a curveball to Rancho Cucamonga's number five hitter), but he decided not to say a word—his instincts told him to leave well enough alone in matters directly relating to the education of the Anointed One. Instead, he sat silently through the inning, a several feet-wide gap between him and J.R. Time to shift gears, Jeff thought as play began in the ninth. He took a drink of Gatorade from a paper cup, then spoke to J.R. without looking at him. "You know what, Mario—"

"Actually, I'm more the Jeff Gordon type, only better looking—and wise of you to associate me with speed," J.R. quipped. North walked Rancho Cucamonga's leadoff hitter after having thrown strikes on his first two pitches.

Jeff rolled his eyes. "Fine, 'Flash'—besides, Gordon's the better comparison anyway." He thought of the tube of toothpaste in his medicine cabinet, the one that had come in a box featuring a glamour shot of Jeff Gordon with a glowing white smile and nubile blondes draped over him. A Rancho Cucamonga pinch hitter singled to right field, putting runners at the corners with nobody out.

"I always knew you were the wise one, gramps," J.R. said.

"Very good, Grasshopper." Jeff wondered if school teachers ever felt like instructing their students in a non-traditional way, maybe keeping a varnished hickory paddle tucked into a drawer in their desks, to be used on, say, the English classroom's version of J.R. Gold. High Desert's manager pulled North and brought in Easterly, who got the first Rancho Cucamonga hitter he faced to pop out on the infield on a pitch outside the strike zone but that the hitter had chased because Easterly had stayed ahead in the count, something Jeff had talked to him about in the locker room before the night's game. Way to keep him guessing, Easterly, Jeff thought as the shortstop cradled the ball in his glove. He spoke to J.R.

106

"Mind if I ask what you had for lunch today?"

"Looking to change your diet—maybe add a few miles per hour to your fastball?" J.R. asked.

"No, it's just that your breath practically knocked me flat when I came to the mound to screw your head on straight—you been eating more of that diseased Texas beef your old man raises down on the South Fork?" It felt good to toss back what J.R. liked to sling. Robidoux, too eager to begin a game-ending double play, muffed a grounder to second, allowing the hitter to reach first and loading the bases. At least he kept the ball in front of him, held the runner at third, Jeff thought.

"Touché, Teach," J.R. said. "If you're asking whether I had the usual, then yes, I certainly did." He smacked his lips. "Amazing how tasty a sick longhorn can be."

Jeff wasn't surprised. He hadn't seen the Anointed One eat anything but fast food since they broke camp in Arizona. "Sheesh, I know the meal money down here isn't going to keep you nibbling on filet mignon every day, but with that signing bonus, you ought to break the bank every once in awhile." Easterly's first pitch with the bases loaded was a strike. "You might at least ask them to hold the onions on your Happy Meal—do you actually kiss the future Miss Texas with that mouth?"

Jeff was surprised to actually see J.R. blush, faintly, before replying in characteristic fashion. "It's not my sweet breath she likes," he said.

Jeff chuckled. There's no end to this guy, he thought. On a two-two fastball, Easterly threw a heavy sinker that the Rancho Cucamonga hitter hit on the ground to the shortstop, who fielded the ball cleanly and shoveled it to second, where Robidoux's cleats brushed the bag as he made the pivot and fired the ball to first to complete the double play that ended the game. Yes, Jeff thought. Just like that. "C'mon, 'Flash,'" Jeff said, climbing the dugout steps toward the field where the team had begun to congregate on the infield, offering handshakes and knuckle bumps. "Easterly saved your 'W'—time to give some props." Jeff loved the feeling that accompanied such a gathering after a win—the sense of camaraderie that passed between the players, the pleasant buzz in the air as a satisfied home crowd began heading for the exits. Even the tinny canned ballpark music sounded better as he returned to the dugout and walked down the tunnel to the locker room.

Jeff showered and tossed his personal effects into his duffel. He

107

whistled a few bars of Steve Earle's "Another Town"—even an overnight bus trip to Stockton didn't seem as bad following a win. He had just pulled his polo shirt over his head and grabbed his duffel when High Desert's third base coach came to his locker. "Skipper wants to see you in his office."

Jeff walked through the thick locker room air, a strange mixture of cologne, body odor, and rusting metal, to the manager's office. When he stepped into the office, the refrigerated air from the rattling window air conditioner hit like a wet blanket. J.R., in t-shirt and sliding shorts, sat on the couch that spilled foam rubber stuffing through its frayed seams. Jeff returned his sardonic smile before speaking to the manager. "You wanted me, skip?"

"Have a seat," he said, waving a hand toward a mid-1950's vintage office chair. Jeff had a sense of what was coming—he appreciated Bowie's approach. Jeff chalked it up to the fact that the manager had himself been a player—not a spectacular performer, but a reliable utility infielder who'd earned the nickname Scrap Metal. "Boys," he said to both Jeff and J.R.—a greeting that Jeff certainly didn't mind— "you've both done your jobs admirably this last month and a half." J.R.'s statistics certainly showed his brilliance—an ERA under 3.00, an average of just over a strikeout per inning, a 6-1 record—and Jeff knew that a manager like Scrap Metal recognized the value of what he'd done with the Anointed One. "And I just wanted to let you both know that I just got off the phone with Ray Daubach. You boys are headed for Huntsville."

Jeff watched J.R. pump his fist and listened to his war whoop crash against the cheap wood paneling of the office. Jeff also caught the look Scrap Metal shot J.R.—an ironic mixture of amusement and *give me a swig of Pepto Bismol straight*" before he made eye contact with the manager. The curl of his upper lip as he shook his head told Jeff more than anything he could put into words.

Fifth Inning

Four things had dominated Jeff's thoughts that spring—educating the Anointed One, Daubach's carrot on the stick, Big Al's news about retirement, and Carolyn. All four followed him across the better part of the continent when he and the J.R. made the jump to Double A ball in

108

Huntsville, followed him as the days lengthened and an Alabama summer brought its inevitable heat and humidity. At the ballpark, he focused on coaching and his thoughts of returning to the Show. In the locker room, the dugout, the bullpen, and on the mound, Jeff found himself growing into the role of teacher/mentor, a role he came to realize suited him. In addition to his bringing along the Anointed One, Jeff found himself advising the other young pitchers on the Huntsville staff, pointing out glitches in their mechanics, talking them through hypothetical situations they would face, even offering advice on how to carry themselves professionally on and off the field. Jeff was sure that other coaches had covered this ground with these pitchers before, but there was something in the way Jeff communicated with these players that made it stick. Even J.R.'s penchant for sarcasm directed at "Gramps" slowed down—though he kept it up just enough to remind Jeff that he was still a kid possessing a healthy measure of the inner jerk.

That wasn't to say coaching had become a walk in the park for Jeff. The hardest thing in the world for him was watching J.R. on the mound making mistakes that he could get away with in the low minors, but would certainly bite him in the ass when he hit the big time. And more than once, the pitcher still living inside Jeff developed itches that couldn't be scratched. He wanted, if only for a single outing, to take to the mound with Luckow moxie and the Gold arm. And when Jeff did take to the mound, it typically meant eating up an inning or two in games that were entirely out of reach. That pitcher inside threw tantrums, making Jeff's brain literally hum with its profanity-laced tirades directed at the gods of baseball who'd seen fit to place him in a thirty-two year-old body with a left arm that simply couldn't do the things asked of it. During one of these infrequent outings, Jeff made the mistake of looking into the dugout at a smirking J.R. Gold who walked to the water cooler like an old man needing hip replacement sugery, leaning on a bat as if it were a cane. Seeing this, Jeff went to the rosin bag, bounced it across his pitching hand, and threw it—hard—to the damp earth near the back of the mound where it made a sick-wet *thud*. He then ended the inning by striking out the next hitter on three pitches—two agonizingly slow change-ups (the first in on the hands, the second painting the black on the outside corner) and a fastball that looked twice as fast as it really was because of the change-ups he'd used to set it up. Take that, you little prick, he thought as he walked back toward the dugout. When he reached the warning track, he looked J.R. in the eye and faked a limp. The Anointed One removed his cap and kowtowed to Jeff. Bastard, he thought.

Away from the ballpark, though, Jeff found himself thinking—far more than he wanted to—about his father's one-two punch. He'd talked about Jeff needing to leave the game on his own terms, but in no way could Jeff see himself ever walking away. If there wasn't a place for him stateside (coaching, he reminded himself), maybe he could still play somewhere else—hook up with a team in Mexico or Japan or the new Australian League. It wasn't that he didn't try to prepare himself to walk away from the game, didn't try to see the truth of what his father had said about life on the farm, didn't try to understand that his father had reached the end of the line and wanted, more than anything, to see the land that had been in the Luckow family for more than a century stay in the family. It was just that all these these late night rationalizations, as he slumped in an uncomfortable seat on the team bus speeding through the countryside on the way to the next three-game set, were merely intellectual exercises that made perfect sense in his head, but they were ultimately hollow when he tried to feel their weight in his stomach.

And Carolyn—Jeff had, he thought, put to rest the issue of what had happened in those months following high school graduation. But knowing that she was there, in Gillett, and would be there should he fulfill Big Al's wish— what was he supposed to say when he bumped into her some Sunday in church or in the aisle of the grocery store? From the tone of Big Al's weekly phone calls, she wasn't merely looking to stay for a few months before moving on to who knew what else and where else. It had taken Jeff nearly three years to stop thinking of her almost daily, to stop hearing in his dreams the cold, metallic timbre of her voice over a pay phone and finally take her final Christmas present to him—beautiful as it was—to a pawn shop where, to the best of his knowledge, it still sat, gathering dust alongside remnants of other people's lives.

What kept Jeff going through those years had been, simply, baseball. Even the small, weather-scarred parks in West Virginia or Pennsylvania or upstate New York, where ancient wooden seats no longer held the flaking green paint on their pitted surfaces, were an escape to a reality that felt better than all he would have had to accept in Gillett. It was a reality where a promotion to the next rung on the ladder might be only two or three decent outings away and where the cathedrals that housed major league clubs might await two or three decent seasons down the line. And the physical sensations of playing and simply being on the diamond—his muscles and tendons stretching, perspiration cooling his skin on a summer night, newly-mown bluegrass rolling in endless green waves—were enough to push out of his mind anything but playing his part. No matter how insignificant it seemed, the new stories developed every night in front of a few hundred fans.

Jeff had begun dating again after a time—young co-eds home for summer vacation, or local women who worked on the assembly lines of the factories in the second-rate rust belt towns of the low minors. These women were generally pleasant, but in a featureless way. They filled a role, feeding certain appetites in hopes of latching onto their own ticket to the proverbial big time. Nothing more, nothing less. But they never made his head swim the way Carolyn had over a decade earlier, never reached right into him to the place that Carolyn could find and hold without even thinking about it, the place she could touch in a way that made him feel he'd never want or need anyone else ever again. After the seasons and their brief hook-ups ended, though, Jeff never felt the need to write or call these women, never felt a need to ask them to travel to Wisconsin, to the farm, to meet Big Al or to, literally, take a roll in the hay. Typically, they never felt compelled to call or write Jeff either. They didn't beg him to stay and share the rent on their single-bedroom flats or go with them to their college towns and claim space on a futon in a studio apartments.

After Big Al mentioned Carolyn, though, she began appearing in Jeff's thoughts. At first, she was only on the fringes—almost like the tinny canned music pumped into the ballparks as players warmed up for the game, there as background noise only. But before long, when Jeff was away from the ballpark, she always seemed to be there: the hint of her laugh in the voice of a waitress, the bounce of her hair on women in commercials for household cleaning products as he watched The Price Is Right to kill time. It seemed that almost every woman he saw over the space of several days in early June wore a flowered sundress.

And then came Little League Day at Huntsville Memorial Stadium.

The team had invited area Little League teams to attend a Sunday afternoon game, offering one-dollar seats and discounted concessions for the young players. As part of the promotion, the team drew the names of twenty-five Little Leaguers—one for every member of the Huntsville roster—and invited them onto the field prior to the game to play catch with a member of the Huntsville squad. Jeff had to laugh when he saw who J.R. had been paired with—an overweight ten year-old with Coke-bottle glasses and a lisp that sent a spray of saliva over the front of J.R.'s uniform when he introduced himself. Then a member of Huntsville's front office brought over Jeff's "Little Big Leaguer" (as the team had billed the lucky twenty five).

At first, the boy seemed physically unremarkable—average height, average build—but when Jeff looked at him more closely, he couldn't help but notice the spray of tiny freckles spread over the boy's nose and the loose, red-brown hair that curled out from beneath his mesh cap. And when Jeff looked into the boy's green eyes, he could have sworn that he was looking into a mirror. His eyes sloped down beneath heavy brows in the same way Jeff's did, seemed to look closely not only at him, but into him—in a manner that simultaneously searched for something in Jeff even as already knew what it would find. And as the boy looked at him, Jeff heard Carolyn's voice in the back of his mind: *"When you look at me, it's like you're so...there."*

For a long moment, Jeff didn't know what to say as he stared back at his assigned Little Big Leaguer. "You okay, mister?" the boy asked.

Jeff felt himself nod. "Yeah...I'm okay," he said. "Sorry—my mind wandered there for a second." When Jeff heard himself speak, it was as if the sound of his voice came back to him through heavy gauze. He introduced himself.

"Cool," the boy said. "I'm Brandon."

Jeff watched Brandon slip his right hand into his mitt. And a southpaw, too, Jeff thought. He felt an almost electrical charge wash over his body, exiting through his fingertips, leaving him feel weak. Jeff felt a trickle of sweat run down his ribs.

"Say," Brandon said, "Didn't you pitch for, like, a month with Cream City a few years ago?"
An image of Camden Yards, site of his major league debut, flashed through Jeff's mind. "You got it," he said. "How in the world did you know that?" He placed his fingers around the ball in the pocket of his mitt and tossed it to Brandon.

"Before my family moved here last summer," Brandon said, his mitt closing around the ball, "we lived near Baltimore."

"An O's fan?" Jeff asked. His body still felt like a large rubber band as they continued tossing the ball back and forth.

"Big time," Brandon said. "And I was at the park this one Saturday afternoon in September—"

"Lord, don't tell me you saw that disaster," Jeff said, groaning as he caught Brandon's throw. He closed his eyes for a moment and shook his head, picturing an opposite-field home run ball crashing into the red brick warehouse beyond the right field wall—the final pitch Jeff had thrown in the first of his three major league outings, all of them similar to that September debut when he'd given up six runs on five hits and a pair of walks in just two-thirds of an inning.

"We were like three rows up from the dugout," Brandon said. "You looked a little ticked off when they took you out of the game, like maybe you didn't feel too good."

"I didn't," Jeff said. His stomach involuntarily lurched, and he tasted something bitter in the back of his throat. "That was one ugly outing."

"Hey, it's okay," Brandon said. Jeff saw him blushing beneath the visor of his mesh cap. The boy's next throw came in at an odd angle, nearly getting past Jeff. "I'm sorry if I…"

"No, no—it's okay," Jeff said. "It's actually kind of cool that you knew that." And it is, Jeff thought. Nice to be remembered.

The game of catch continued for a few more minutes, their conversation sticking to predictable topics—Jeff asking Brandon about his Little League season and what subjects he liked in school, Brandon asking about which major league parks Jeff had visited and what it was like to pitch against players like Cal Ripken, Jr. After the games of catch came to a halt, the Huntsville players autographed the balls for their Little Big Leaguers before they were ushered back to their seats. Jeff scolded himself for the feeling growing in his chest.

Jeff watched Brandon wave back at him from the grandstand and thought of Big Al, of the times they'd had a catch alongside the farmhouse after milking and chores—it wasn't something they did often, but those lazy throws had never failed to make him feel closer to his father. And he thought of Carolyn, of how they'd driven to Shawano early in their Senior year to see *Field of Dreams*. Jeff had never seen a film like that—he'd never had a movie that made him feel as if part of him had been physically pried open, had never had a movie, just shadows on a screen, make him cry. Seemingly from nowhere, Carolyn had produced a tissue when the tears began to slide down Jeff's cheeks as Costner's Ray Kinsella threw the ball back and forth with the younger version of his father. They sat through the credits, not speaking. Carolyn gently pulled his head downward so that his cheek rested against her chest

113

just beneath her collarbone. Jeff was crying, silently. He remembered feeling so sad and good and embarrassed and safe. Carolyn stroked his hair, the slight rise and fall of her chest comforting him as he sat with her in the darkness, foggy pictures of ballparks and the farm and Carolyn flashing across a movie screen in his mind. Jeff didn't know what they meant, but the pictures felt big, felt somehow important, as if he had been given glimpses of an indeterminate future.

J.R. brought Jeff back to Huntsville. "Where is she?" he asked.

Jeff blinked several times in rapid succession. "Where's who?" he asked as J.R. intently surveyed the stands.

"The babe, gramps." J.R. squinted as he looked down the right field line. "The way you were standing there just staring like that, I figured that maybe you'd seen some hot little number. Is that her?" he asked, pointing to a field level box where an attractive woman in a halter-top had just taken a bite of a hot dog. "Thought maybe I'd break the bank and spring for some Viagra for you. Little blue miracles."

Jeff looked at the Anointed One, raised a single eyebrow, and sighed. J.R. smiled at the woman in the halter top and winked. Miracles, thought Jeff. Miracles indeed.

Sixth Inning

Huntsville killed El Paso on Little League Day. By the seventh inning, they already led by twelve runs. Jeff pitched the final two innings to save arms for the next day's double-header. El Paso's hitters made good contact against his pitches—none of their six hits were of the cheap variety, and their outs came on well-hit balls that quickly found their way to the fielders. He gave up a run in the eighth (the damage could have been worse had he not managed to get El Paso's clean-up hitter to chase a pitch outside the zone), and he left the bases loaded when the game's final batter hit a long fly ball to the center field warning track.

Jeff was thankful for the blast of air conditioning that hit him as he entered the locker room. He sat down in front of his locker and began peeling off his uniform. He'd just removed a sanitary sock as J.R., naked save for the thick white towel draped over his arm, walked toward him with a look on his face that prompted Jeff to cut him off at the pass. "Not a word, Mario."

"Still don't get it, eh?" J.R. asked. "I thought you'd remember that I'm more the—"

"That's right," Jeff said, lifting his sweat-soaked undershirt up and over his head. "Pardon my Alzheimer's—you're more the Jeff Gordon type."

"Straight up, Gramps. I just wanted to tell you…" J.R. looked around and lowered his voice before he continued, "that you did okay in the eighth, when you got their clean-up hitter. You so totally set him up to go after that pitch."

Christ, Jeff thought, wonders never cease. He looked up at the Anointed One. "Thanks," he said and dropped the undershirt to the floor.

J.R. raised his voice when as he replied, walking toward his locker. "Just too bad they don't make Viagra for the arm."

Jeff shook his head, finished taking off his uniform, and made his way to the shower. Normally he enjoyed the hot spray of the water against his skin and the moist air he inhaled. Showers typically let him just float after the game—to let his mind go wherever it wanted—but today, he barely felt the water, and he couldn't seem to breathe in enough of the humid air. He thought of playing catch before the game, the way, when he looked at Brandon, he saw *his* eyes, saw Carolyn's hair color and her freckles. The boy must have been around twelve, he thought.

As Jeff lathered in the shower, he tried picturing himself as a father—of playing catch, not with a randomly selected Little Leaguer on the diamond of a minor league ballpark, but with a boy possessing his DNA, alongside the farmhouse where he'd grown up, the house that would again become home according to Big Al's plans. For a moment, Jeff thought he could detect the scent of crabapple blossoms in the shower's damp air, the scent that had blown in through his bedroom window in the farmhouse when he was a boy, telling him spring was nearly over and summer was just around the corner. But the scent left Jeff as quickly as it came, and the more he tried to focus on the image of himself and a boy playing catch in the yard, the more gauzy the picture became. The boy became nearly transparent, and Jeff couldn't fix on a precise image of himself. The crabapple blossoms were replaced with the stink of the manure pile blowing up from the south end of the barnyard, When the ghost boy sent one final throw to Jeff, the ball never reached him. It simply vanished, lost wherever dream tosses ultimately land.

Jeff rinsed, turned off the water, and toweled himself dry. He wrapped the heavy cotton towel around his waist and returned to his locker. He sat down again, more tired than he'd been before showering.

The clubhouse boy began making his rounds, distributing mail to the players. He handed Jeff three envelopes. The first had a local return address. The usual, Jeff thought—some minor league clubs attracted a loyal following, so it wasn't unusual to receive an autograph request or a child's "you're my favorite…can you come to my birthday party?" or even the occasional marriage proposal. Today's first letter was written in the large, looping letters of a child who asked for an autograph and had even enclosed an index card and a self-addressed stamped envelope. Jeff grabbed a pen from his locker, scratched his name across the index card, and put it into the return envelope.

The second letter was from a graduate student on the West Coast. The author wrote about his love of baseball and literature, how he was working on a novel whose protagonist was a career minor-leaguer, and how in the course of his research he'd come across Jeff's name and career stats in *Baseball America*. He wanted to interview Jeff to "discover the essence of what makes you keep going, what makes you persevere even though you must surely know, on some level, that you will never attain your dream." Piss off, Jeff thought as he tore the letter in two, then wadded the halves together in a ball that he flung across the room.

Before opening the third letter, Jeff looked at the return address on the envelope. No name—just a street address and a zip code. 54124. Gillett, he thought, but Big Al doesn't write letters. He looked more closely at the handwriting on the envelope—the carefully formed letters, the way each of them slanted to the right at exactly the same angle, the extra curve added to the loop of the "L" in his last name. Jeff felt the hiss of white noise swelling up from somewhere deep inside his head. Cold beads of sweat popped up on the back of his neck. Oh shit, he thought, pulling the neatly folded sheets of paper from the envelope. He took a deep breath and felt a pain in his side. As soon as he read the opening "*Dear Jeff*" and saw the open-ended "r," he knew.

Carolyn.

For a long time—Jeff couldn't be sure how long—he sat there, his head hanging down as his teammates filtered out of the locker room. He tried to focus on the words on the page, but the letters blurred, wouldn't become clear and form words Jeff could begin to comprehend. J.R., cutting a classic figure in his Ralph Lauren duds, stopped by Jeff's locker. "Everything okay?" he asked.

"Uh-huh," Jeff mumbled.

"You look like you just had a Texas longhorn kick you where the sun don't shine," J.R. said.

Jeff simply shook his head.

"You sure you're not having a heart attack, Gramps? No numbness in the extremities or anything like that?"

Jeff looked up at J.R. "Go get yourself a Big Mac, Mario."

J.R. laughed. "Just showing a little genuine human concern."

Jeff grunted. He folded the sheets of Carolyn's letter and slid them back into the envelope. He tossed the envelope onto a shelf in his locker. "I'm okay. Really."

J.R. shrugged. "If you say so. But just remember," he said, wagging his long index finger at Jeff, "'aspirin taken during a heart attack significantly increases the odds of survival.' Learned that from a Bayer commercial."

"Nice," Jeff said. "I'll remember that. Now scram." J.R. raised an eyebrow and shrugged before he turned and walked toward the exit.

The clubhouse boy had begun collecting the towels that lay scattered across the locker room floor. Jeff stood, slowly, feeling strength reluctantly re-enter his limbs, and took the towel from around his waist and tossed it into the rolling laundry cart. Jeff dressed carefully, deliberately. After tying his shoes, he stood as straight as he could and breathed deeply, letting the air completely fill his lungs before he exhaled, forcing out the air in an almost violent rush. He felt...old. Old and tired. He picked up Carolyn's letter from the shelf in his locker and started removing the pages, but stopped and tucked them back in. You're probably going to want a good, stiff drink after reading this, he thought. Save it. Jeff folded the envelope in half and slipped it into his shirt pocket. Rather than walking out the exit toward the parking lot, Jeff walked up the tunnel that led to the dugout. He crossed the dugout floor, careful to avoid the husks of sunflower seeds and wads of gum and streaks of viscous brown tobacco juice, and climbed the steps toward the field.

The grounds crew—three men whose beer bellies spilled out over their belts—was busy tending the diamond. Jeff stepped over the low wall alongside the dugout and sat in a box seat, watching the grounds crew at work. One of the men drove a lawn tractor, dragging the infield dirt with a heavy metal contraption that resembled a mattress box spring stripped of padding and fabric. He drove carefully, covering every square inch of the dirt, erasing cleat marks and the streaks left by players who'd slid into base.

Jeff shifted his attention to the second member of the grounds crew, who held a hose attached to a hidden spigot behind the pitcher's mound. After the man on the tractor had erased any sign of life from a section of dirt, the second worker sprayed a fine mist from the nozzle, sweeping back and forth across the dirt, careful not to over-saturate any section of the infield. With each sweep of the hose, the dirt grew darker, going from the light color of beach sand baked in the sun to a deep, rich brown that reminded Jeff of the farm fields after Big Al had plowed.

The third member of the crew worked around home plate. From a plastic five-gallon pail, he poured dirt over the areas of the batter's boxes where players had kicked away the earth as they dug in at the plate. With a steel rake, he carefully worked the ground around the plate, breaking up any clumps, making sure any hollows had been filled, raking the soil all around the plate to the same consistency. When he finished with the rake, Jeff watched him lug, with some difficulty, the next tool he would use. It was chest-high—a wooden handle attached to a flat steel disk—and he lifted it straight up before letting the combination of gravity, his strength, and aim bring it down on the earth with a *thudslap* that echoed softly off the stadium's empty seats. When he'd finished tamping the soil, the worker with the hose walked toward the plate and sprayed the area, making the dirt turn the same shade of brown as the rest of the infield's skin.

Jeff watched them finish their work, then looked down at his hands. They were as big as his father's, but they didn't look the same. No matter how hard Big Al scrubbed, he couldn't erase the years of grease and loamy Wisconsin soil that accumulated in the ridges and creases of his skin, in the valleys around his fingernails. When Jeff was still in school, his father's hands had been a source of embarrassment. Jeff felt uncomfortable going to church and seeing Big Al exchange handshakes, hated having him come to school functions where, Jeff thought, people who didn't understand farming might whisper among themselves about how Big Al Luckow couldn't even clean himself properly. But now, sitting in the empty stadium—watching the grounds crew finish tending the earth—Jeff felt pride at the thought of his father's stained hands. He examined his own hands at arm's length—long-fingered, nails closely clipped, veins a faint blue web beneath skin still faintly wrinkled from his locker room shower. Now, tried to imagine them as farmer's hands, the land itself embedded a living, moving part of his flesh. With each hand, he spread the fingers wide, feeling the tendons

118

and muscles stretch. The tendons and muscles in his left hand so easily cradled the circumference of a baseball, and those in his right hand had snapped closed the leather of his glove to snare grounders and liners. They were tasks that had become as natural as breathing. Jeff tried to imagine them performing the tasks that were a part of Big Al's rituals, the daily chores that never went away, the jobs that cycled along with the seasons.

Jeff set his jaw and swallowed hard, let his hands return to their normal posture, and closed his eyes for several seconds. When he opened them, he saw the scoreboard lights blink out. The early evening haze diffused the remaining sunlight, allowing him to look directly at the sun hanging like a gopher ball just above the top row of outfield bleachers. Jeff stood up, went back through the dugout, and began a slow, silent walk toward the parking lot.

Jeff found J.R. sitting in front of the television in the cramped living room of their furnished two-bedroom apartment. Grease-stained McDonald's bags and empty French fry cartons littered the floor in front of the couch. The Anointed One was playing a baseball video game. Digitized organ music and the hiss of simulated crowd noise came out the television speakers. J.R. whooped. "Oh yeah," he said, gesturing toward the screen with his controller, "no way big, bad Barry handles the high heat."

"Studying for your finals, I see?" Jeff asked. He went into the kitchen and pulled a Styrofoam container from the refrigerator. Leftover lo mein. He put it in the microwave.

"You know it, gramps," J.R. said. The crowd noise swelled from the television.

Jeff didn't have to twist J.R.'s arm to get him to buy one of the slick new video game systems and a baseball simulation game. Jeff had purchased an earlier version of the system during the off-season three years earlier. At first, it had been something to bring baseball to the months that stretched between the end of one season and the start of the next, but the more Jeff played the game, the more he realized that the simulation was rather sophisticated and, to a degree, accurate. The digital players looked—and more importantly, performed—like their major league counterparts. The computerized Jeff Bagwell stood with his feet spread wide and hit for power. The digital Ichiro Suzuki covered the plate better than any hitter and sprayed hits to all fields. Barry Bonds

119

crowded the plate, daring a pitcher to come inside against him. Jeff came
to view the game as a way to mentally prepare himself, to learn hitters'
tendencies, just in case the call should come. He started spending hours
in front of the television, jotting notes into an old spiral-bound notebook.
Big Al, feeling either neglected or pissed off that he couldn't watch *Will
and Grace* (Jeff found his father's crush on Debra Messing almost
charming), actually tried to unhook the system from the television. But
for all the mechanical adeptness he brought to repairing a haybine or a
John Deere, he couldn't figure out the maze of cords and cables Jeff had
arranged behind the old Zenith console.

That spring, when Daubach dangled the carrot in front of Jeff, he figured
that any tool at his disposal was fair game. So shortly after being
assigned to the minor league complex, he'd taken J.R. to an electronics
superstore and "encouraged" him to spend some of his signing bonus.

    The microwave beeped. Jeff removed the re-heated Chinese food.
He felt Carolyn's letter in his pocket and went to the refrigerator for a
beer before going to the living room. He sat in the old Barcalounger. "So
how'd you whiff Sammy Sosa tonight?" Jeff asked.

    "Got him thinking inside, then made him go fishin'—you'd think
for being one of those Cuban boat people, he'd be better at that."

    Jeff shook his head. Lordy, lordy. He began chewing a mouthful
of lo mein. It was sour. "Sammy's from Puerto Rico."

    "Same difference," J.R. said. "Some island south of Florida,
right?"

    "That's right," Jeff said. He set the Styrofoam container next to
the beer on the chipped formica end table beside the chair. "You're from
Texas."

    "What's that supposed to mean?" J.R. asked. He didn't take his
eyes off the screen. 'He' was Curt Schilling on the game, about to deliver
a pitch.

    "One of Dubya's model schools…it all makes sense," Jeff said.
He pushed forward against the chair's arms and the footrest creaked into
place.

    "At least he does a better job of running America than he did the
Rangers," J.R. said. The computerized Fred McGriff hit a double to right
against his Schilling. The crowd roared. "Damn."

    Jeff laughed. "That's open to debate. And remember—
McGriff's a low ball hitter…you put it right in his wheelhouse."

    J.R. didn't bother responding to Jeff, though he did look back at him as if to say to Jeff, "hey, it's my game—I'll figure it out." Jeff wanted to say something more but thought better of it. That was something he wasn't always good at doing, letting the silence speak for itself, convey its lesson in the unspoken words that fulfilled their potential only by remaining unspoken. Jeff wasn't as good at it as some coaches he'd had along the line. Or as good as Big Al. He remembered the time when Big Al had sent him out to the field by the railroad tracks to side rake the windrows—the first time his dad had sent him to do the job unsupervised. Jeff had stopped the tractor and side rake just short of the outside windrow and cranked down the teeth of the side rake—rows of metal prongs mounted to metal bars stretched between angled steel disks that spun as the tractor pulled the contraption. Thrilled to be out there, alone for the first time, no Big Al riding shotgun on the fender of the old "Poopy John," Jeff had taken off like a bat out of hell. He was whistling tunes he'd heard on the radio, thinking about the ballgame in Cream City Big Al had promised him after they'd finished the second crop, and generally enjoying life as he circled the field.

As he came around the bend at the southwest corner of the field on his third circuit of the field, Jeff saw Big Al standing just inside the fence, his Jacques Seed cap pulled low, his biceps filling up his frayed shirtsleeves. As Jeff came closer to Big Al, he slowed the tractor and finally came to a stop. Big Al didn't say a word to Jeff—just let his eyes slowly travel from Jeff back to the side rake and then to the windrows Jeff had driven over in his circuits of the field's perimeter.

Jeff immediately noticed what Big Al had seen—that none of the rows had been turned over by the side rake. Jeff had lowered the teeth of the side rake, but he'd forgotten to engage the gear alongside the side rake's wheel, the gear that allowed the steel disks to turn, causing the teeth to lift and flip the windrows of cut hay. The outside windrows were a mess. The teeth had scraped against the cut alfalfa in places, but without turning, they had done nothing but drag the hay and drop it in clumps now scattered haphazardly along the windrows.

Jeff couldn't believe he hadn't seen what was going on. He climbed off Poopy John, and avoiding Big Al's eyes, walked around behind the side rake and stepped down on the lever that engaged the gears. Big Al looked at Jeff, nodded, then turned around and began the walk through the pasture toward home.

Sitting in the Barcalounger, Jeff still felt the heat blooming in his cheeks. He watched J.R. playing the video game. It was odd to watch the man-child carry on a dialogue with the pixels sketching out an imaginary ballgame on the television screen. Jeff leaned back in the chair, let his head sink into the headrest. The Styrofoam container of Chinese food sat on an end table, growing cold, the open bottle of beer next to it, growing warm. He wanted the foam rubber beneath the scarred leather surface to mold itself to his contours, to hold his body so that his mind could simply drift, but he couldn't get comfortable. Annoyed, Jeff sat back up and rubbed his forehead. He reached into his shirt pocket and removed the folded envelope he'd brought home from the ballpark. He knew that he needed to read the letter, but he somehow didn't feel ready; he'd hoped to put it off—like getting a shot or filing taxes. Reading it, he knew, meant confronting things he'd rather not think about, at least not now.

True, he'd been thinking of Carolyn often since he'd last spoken with Big Al, but until the letter arrived, that's all it had been—thinking of her. Thinking of the time they'd spent together, of nearly everything but the one time Jeff wished he'd been able to keep his mouth shut. Graduation. When Carolyn had inhaled the fragrance of the lilac blossoms Jeff had brought her just before they left for the ceremony, he hadn't been surprised by the tears. Such gestures typically found her soft spot, and with commencement just an hour away, with the big future they'd planned just around the corner, tears seemed somehow fitting. Jeff remembered how he smiled at her, how he felt so full of…tenderness. Optimism.

Love.

It had been all of those things combined. And he remembered the way Carolyn looked back at him, the way she smiled. He saw something in her eyes that he couldn't define—a new look, one that, for an instant, made his heart jump up into his throat. That feeling returned after the commencement ceremony ended and Carolyn pulled him aside in the hallway behind the gymnasium, into the alcove where the door to the band room was propped open, and said, "Jeff, we've got something to talk about."

"Talk is cheap," he said, his hand running over the slick fabric of the graduation gown, then sliding up the wide sleeve. Her skin was cold beneath his palm, covered with a thousand tiny goosebumps. He felt her shiver.

Carolyn stepped away from Jeff. "I mean really talk." She paused. "Something…happened."

In the measured tone of her voice, Jeff felt the weight of the two

122

words send her shiver through him. Through the door of the band room, he saw members of the band putting away their instruments. Chris Lewicki placed a tuba into what looked like a small coffin, and Cybelle Egan pulled apart her clarinet piece by piece and nestled the parts into the velvet-lined compartments of its case. Jeff and Carolyn walked toward the exit and stepped through the door toward a small patch of lawn tucked behind cedar hedges. Jeff felt a crunch beneath his shoe. He stepped away and saw the remains of a June bug. They'd been especially thick that year, and looking up, he saw more than he could've counted flying their cumbersome paths through the stark glow of the security light.

Carolyn stood along the hedge. She'd taken off her graduation robe and was tugging at a thread poking out from a seam at the waist of her skirt. She shifted her weight from one foot to another, and when she spoke, she didn't look up at Jeff—she just kept picking at that thread. "Do you remember how in *Huck Finn* Aunt Sally can't comprehend that Huck isn't Tom and Tom isn't Sid—she's all surprised, but when the shock wears off she's about the happiest person around?"

"I remember talking about it in class—I never actually read the last half of the book," Jeff said. He ran a finger over the leather case holding the diploma that certified he was a newly-minted graduate of Gillett High School. "What about it—are you about to tell me that you're not really named Carolyn? That you're Carolyn's third cousin Clarissa and that you really don't care about me in the slightest but were only stringing me along the last eight-and-a-half months? Something you did for a good laugh?" Jeff laughed, but his voice sounded dry, and it cracked in the damp June air.

Carolyn barely held back a groan and finally stopped picking at the thread. She made eye contact with Jeff, the first time she'd done so since they'd taken their places in the processional line before the ceremony. "I'm pregnant, Jeff."

Jeff surprised himself. He began to laugh—a full belly laugh that went on for too long. It echoed off the brick exterior of the school, cut through the glow of the security light, and trailed off into the black sky. He felt tears begin to trace hot paths down his face, felt the pain of laughter in his stomach, and looked at Carolyn. She was a blur, and he blinked several times to bring her into focus. "You can't be," he said.

"Almost two months," she said. "I didn't want to say anything until I knew for sure."

"But we—"

"Accidents happen," Carolyn said. She began pulling at the thread again. It let loose, and in an instant, she held a length of thread that trailed from the now-open seam. "Shit," she said.

Jeff's mind froze, filled with an empty white light, and then the images came in momentary flashes. He pictured his parents at the kitchen table, their faces like contorted rubber Halloween masks. He saw friends glancing at him out the corner of their eyes as they whispered to one another behind the backs of their hands. His high school coach, Coach C, shuffled away from him, muttering, shaking his head. The scouts, who'd come to the games he pitched with their radar guns and their thick notebooks in tow, tore several sheets of paper away from the spiral binding, then tore them neatly in half. He could see his own baseball glove drying out, the supple leather bleaching; thirsty for neat's-foot oil, the laces were splitting, allowing the fingers to overlap. Carolyn, her hair streaked with gray, punched the keys of a register at the grocery store. And he could see himself, operating one of the hydraulic presses at Linwood, compressing thin pine veneers to form four-by-eight sheets of half-inch plywood. As the slide show went on, Jeff felt a thought forming, an idea, but before he could allow it to take shape completely, he spoke. "Look," he said, "this certainly wasn't in the plans."

Carolyn gave him her *you're telling me*? look. "These things rarely are." She ran the palms of her hand over the bare skin of her arms.

Jeff felt the warmth in his cheeks fade, felt the pain of laughter in his stomach turn into a different, deeper kind of pain. Unable to make eye contact, he looked at the open seam. "What about college for you? Are you...?"

"I don't know," she said. "Seems kind of hard now, doesn't it?"

"And what about..." Jeff said. He allowed the unfinished phrase to hang in the space between them. Earlier that day, Coach C had told him the scouts were definitely interested—that he wouldn't go in the upper rounds of the coming draft, but that he'd definitely be selected. Coach had told him they liked his approach, the way he worked.

Jeff looked into the sky. Beyond the glare of the security lights, he could see the moon, nearly full. His eyes slowly traced downward. Looking along the streets leading away from the school, he could see the shapes of things faintly illuminated by the moonlight—the oak trees along the sidewalks, the plastic bags of garbage left out for the next day's pick-up, the silvered silhouette of rooflines stretching toward, but not quite reaching, the horizon. Above the roofs, Jeff saw the smokestacks of

Linwood. The smoke that spilled from them twisted with an odd life as it snaked into the night. In the damp air, Jeff smelled the faint odor of manure that a farmer had spread on his field earlier in the day. Jeff spoke before precisely framing his thought, before choosing the words that conveyed exactly what he wanted to say. "Carolyn, I can't let this stop me from…Maybe we should have thought of…this can't stand in the way of—" At the edge of his vision, Jeff saw Carolyn stand straight, saw her body go stiff. He knew that in her mind, Carolyn had already finished his sentence for him.

"Maybe we should have thought about a lot of things," she said.

They stood there for several long, awkward seconds, not looking at each other, not speaking. Jeff heard a June bug slam into the light fixture with a quick, quiet pop. Carolyn turned away from him and walked back into the school. It took Jeff several more seconds to make his feet move, to make them follow her into the building.

As if through cotton, Jeff heard the telephone ring. On the television, Sportscenter played highlights from that day's Cream City game. J.R. answered the call in the kitchen. From the sound of his voice, Jeff could tell his girlfriend back in Texas was on the other end of the line. He hoped that J.R. would have the good sense to go to his room and close the door this time. Jeff looked at the Chinese food on the end table. The sweet-sour sauce had congealed, and the pieces of chicken were shriveled, deformed. Jeff's stomach lurched. From the television, Stuart Scott let loose his trademark "Boooooooo-yahhhh!" Jeff felt the tension in his clenched hands. Looking down, he saw that the once neatly folded envelope containing Carolyn's letter had been crushed and now more closely resembled a baseball minus the interlocking leather pieces of its skin. Jeff smoothed out the envelope and removed the sheets of paper inside. From behind the closed door of J.R.'s bedroom, he heard the Anointed One speaking in a low voice that told Jeff more than he wanted to know. Jeff turned up the volume on the television and unfolded the letter. He took a deep breath and began to read.

Seventh Inning

The September 1 promotion to the majors didn't surprise Jeff— Ray Daubach had remained true to his word. Jeff would have been more surprised if the call-up hadn't happened. After J.R. had dominated hitters for a month at Double A Huntsville, he and Jeff had been promoted to Triple A Indianapolis, student and mentor climbing the ladder together. The Anointed One's flashes of civility became more regular as he saw the bright lights of the big leagues flashing on the horizon and realized that Jeff did indeed hold the keys to the kingdom. Every time he went to the two-seamer instead of the four-seamer against a left-hander, every time he made a hitter expecting heat look foolish screwing himself into the dirt chasing a change-up, every time he didn't show up an opponent by going into histrionics after a strike out, he was one day closer to catching a plane to Cream City.

And that plane to Cream City brought Jeff several states closer to home—a three-hour drive from the Luckow farm, a three hour drive from Carolyn Smits, a three-hour drive from a future that everyone else, it seemed, had sketched out for him.

Much of what Carolyn had related in that first letter hadn't been a surprise. Big Al had given him a rundown of her reasons for returning to Gillett—a divorce, her father's illness, the job that opened up when Sandy Lucht retired at the semester break. Jeff was surprised, though, at Carolyn's knowledge of Big Al's plans—for the farm and for Jeff—and at how open she seemed to the idea of their once again being a part of the same community. "I know there was more than a little turbulence between us when things fell apart," she'd written, "but I'd like to think that time can make some things easier to accept." It had taken her some time, she'd written, to move past everything that had—and hadn't—happened over the last six months they'd been "together," a time when, instead of actually working through the fallout, they'd been half a continent apart.

She wrote that for the longest time, she'd held Jeff responsible for her having done what she did. "I felt," she wrote, "on a fundamental level, that what I was doing was wrong, but my head told me that it was the only chance we had. In reality, I didn't know how impossible, how absolutely and completely impossible, it would make things for us, no matter how much we may have wanted to hold on." When Jeff had read those lines, he found himself nodding in silent agreement, felt the same sensation of sinking in the stomach he'd felt when they exchanged gifts on that final Christmas, knowing that no present could bridge the gap that stretched between them. "But," she wrote, "times change, people change. Since we're both finding our way home again, I thought it only right that

126

we touch base, get reacquainted. Life's hard enough as it is without also being alone in the world."

That had been the final line of the letter, the line that Jeff didn't exactly know how to take. He took several weeks to think about it. He'd never been one to write letters, but he finally managed to scratch out a few paragraphs on a notepad and send the note back to Carolyn in Gillett. He thanked her for her letter, told her that he was still working hard and holding out hope of making the big leagues (though he kept Daubach's carrot-on-a-stick from her, as he still did from his father), and that he looked forward to seeing her once the season was over.

Through his remaining weeks in Huntsville and the nine weeks in Indianapolis, Jeff and Carolyn kept writing—his were always short and consisted of vague responses to Carolyn's cautious inquiries about whether he was looking forward to taking over the farm, whether he might be interested in coaching the high school team ("Mr. Eiseth thinks you might be just the shot in the arm the program needs"), whether Jeff, too, believed in time being able to heal. Jeff knew she was feeling him out and that he was doing the same to her—that theirs was a long-distance dance, like a couple of kids waltzing in a phy ed class, fearing what their bodies might do if they were actually to touch each other.

And in that way, old ties were tried on for size and either accepted or rejected. But while Carolyn's letters showed her moving toward answers she wanted and needed, Jeff found himself moving toward more questions.

J.R.'s first start for Cream City created a sensation in a town that—come September 1—typically shifted its attention to the football team that played one hundred miles to the north. In that game, J.R. threw five innings of no-hit ball against Houston before giving up a scratch single in the sixth. Successive starts brought the national media to cover a last-place team, to see the just-turned nineteen phenom befuddle nearly everyone who stepped into the box to face him. Commentators resurrected the ghosts of the game's past in trying to define his impact—they spoke of Feller's debut in 1936, of Doc Gooden's gaudy splash in his early years with the Mets, of the level of dominance Ryan and Koufax had attained early in their careers, but only after having figured things out. "This kid has no learning curve," said an ESPN talking head. "He pitches as if he were born on the mound."

Jeff wanted no part of the limelight J.R. basked in. He was

content to remain in the shadows, an overlooked, nearly forgotten name on the Cream City roster. He knew the role he'd played in getting the Anointed One to the Show. He knew that the right people noticed, and he knew that the proverbial carrot was within his reach. Ray Daubach had taken him to dinner at the Pfister Hotel—a far cry from their meeting at Cactus Jack's months earlier—and told him that there would be a place for him in the organization after he'd "shaken things up a bit" after the end of the season. He hinted that he wasn't going to stand pat with the manager and coaching staff he'd inherited when he'd been named GM role just before the opening of Spring Training.

That dinner had taken place at the beginning of Cream City's season-ending home stand. And for that last week and a half of the season, Jeff wrestled with how he would tell his father that he wouldn't—couldn't—take over the farm. He also struggled with how he would tell Carolyn that, certain things were perhaps better left to the past, were too complicated to resurrect and too dangerous to revive, pleasant as it might be to think of rediscovering something that youth and impulsiveness had prevented from reaching ever-after.

And then what seemed like half of Gillett came to Cream City on the season's final day.

Jeff had known that Big Al and Carolyn would attend the game. "You have about as much chance of seeing me pitch as you do of seeing the sun set in the east," he'd told them, but they insisted on being there anyway. So when he stepped onto the field during pre-game warm-ups, he looked for them in the seats they'd told him they'd finagled from Cream City's front office: field-level, next to the home dugout. What he saw was an entire block of familiar faces, several dozen residents of his hometown. Some of them held a large banner proclaiming "Gillett's Good Luck(ow) Charm—Welcome Home Jeff." They all cheered as he walked toward them. Jeff saw Mr. Eiseth, wearing the red and black cap of the Gillett Tigers, flashing him a thumbs-up and the toothy smile fringed by his wide, elegant mustache. Sandy Lucht, her hair swept up as always in the style that required weekly visits to the beauty shop, clapped rapidly, her small hands a flurry of polite, proper applause. Jeff recognized old classmates and employees of the shops that lined Main Street. He saw Pastor Kamke from St. John's and Annie, the clerk from Owen's Fine Foods he'd come to know during the off-season. Even deaf Dickie Miller was there, clutching a paper cup of beer and babbling incoherently before speaking the only discernable word he was capable of producing—"Miller."

And in the front row, at field level, flanked by Lois Schmidt and Lloyd Kirsch, stood a beaming Big Al, predictably in his plaid shirt and polyester pants, and Carolyn. It was the first time Jeff had actually seen her since that final Christmas. She'd stopped coming home after she got married, and Jeff hadn't seen a purpose in seeking her out in the suburb of the Twin Cities where she lived and taught high school English. His mouth went dry and he felt the same stomach flutters he had when they swam in the river beneath the moonlight years before. Her hair was still the same rich, red-brown he remembered, her smile still pleasantly a degree to the left of center, her complexion still tan, especially against the bright white of her simple cotton shirt, her nose still peppered with a faint spray of freckles.

Jeff was surprised by his father's rare display of public emotion. Big Al opened his arms and hugged Jeff, pulling him close. Jeff could feel the strength in his father's arms as they encircled him, could feel the weight of his hands as he gently thumped him on the back. "Just you and Carolyn, eh?" Jeff asked in a low voice. He could smell the spicy scent of his father's aftershave lotion and felt like an eight year-old again.

"You're not exactly the prodigal son, but your coming back has certainly stirred things up anyway," Big Al said.

His father's embrace finally relaxed and Jeff stepped back. The group was still cheering as he made eye contact with Carolyn. He wanted to slide down a step in her direction, but he couldn't make his feet move. And he felt like he should do something with his hands—maybe reach out to hug her, or, at the very least, shake her hand, but his arms felt like useless appendages as he stood there, taking in her smile. Jeff thought he might be returning the smile, but he wasn't sure, as he couldn't feel anything in his face. For a long, awkward moment he just stood there until Carolyn leaned toward him, smiling, and reached out. She placed one hand on his right elbow, and with her other hand, softly patted his left shoulder three times before letting it rest on his arm. "It's good to see you," Carolyn said.

Jeff could feel the warmth of her hand pass through his jersey and the cotton sleeve of his t-shirt. For a moment, he looked down at her hand, and he noticed she wore a bracelet. Freshwater pearls. "You too," he said. Something scratchy caught in the back of his throat as he spoke.

Jeff was about to say something else when he felt the sharp slap of a baseball mitt against his backside. It was J.R. "Hate to break up this Hallmark moment," he said, "but I gotta have my guru if the baseball gods are gonna keep smiling, right? Wouldn't want to tempt fate."

"Never mess with the magic formula," Jeff said. He stepped away from the stands and let his eyes sweep the familiar faces. In a voice that surprised him, Jeff said to the group, "Thanks—for being here, for everything." These were people who genuinely cared about him. They didn't mind that in thirteen years he'd only spent a month—a single, unsuccessful month—pitching in the majors. They wanted to see him come home, become a permanent member of their world, go to church with them on Sundays, sit with them on the round red vinyl seats at the counter of O.J.'s Midtown Restaurant and have a cup of coffee, a slice of caramel apple pie. They wanted him to share his stories of thirteen years in the wilderness, to teach their boys the fundamentals of the game to bury the Oconto Falls and Wausakees and Peshtigos of the world, showing them just where the Gillett Tigers stood in the scheme of things. They pictured him working the land Big Al had worked the last thirty-five years. Jeff's grandfather had worked for forty before that, tending it, nurturing it, pulling life from it that would fill barns and granaries and corn cribs and take care of "the Girls" as his father affectionately called his Holsteins.

In the bullpen, even J.R.'s early, easy pitches echoed like gunshots off the walls that enclosed it on three sides. To Jeff, the air felt charged—not only by the smothering good will of the Gillett contingent along the first base line, but by the electricity that sparked from the Anointed One's warm-ups. When J.R. cut loose with his first full-velocity pitch, Jeff felt the hairs on the back of his hands stand straight up. "Save some for when it counts," he said.

J.R. shot him a glance, a combination of cocky smarm and self-assurance, and turned back toward his catcher. "So tell me, Gramps," he said, going into his wind-up and hurling another fastball. "The woman by the dugout—she the one?" He took catcher's return throw and went into his motion.

"Yup," Jeff said. He stood, arms crossed, watching J.R., checking his mechanics, watching to make sure he didn't overstride and drag his arm through the delivery. For a moment, Jeff wondered why he'd bothered sharing the bare-bones version of his history with Carolyn with, of all people, J.R. "Let's see the curve, Mario."

J.R.'s next pitch would have turned Babe Ruth's knees to jelly.

"She's kinda hot for an old chick," he said.

Jeff spit. He looked out past the short fence that separated the bullpen from the field. In the stands, near the dugout, he watched Carolyn chatting to the people around her, watched his father standing with his chest puffed out, using big gestures as he spoke. Jeff let his eyes sweep the stands, up toward the press box behind home plate, where Ray Daubach stood in the open window of his private suite, looking toward the bullpen where Cream City's future prepared for the final game of the season, a contest that meant everything and nothing. Jeff couldn't gauge his facial expression from that distance, but he could read the general manager's body language—he leaned forward, his arms supporting the considerable bulk of his upper body, looking for all the world like a king surveying his kingdom. Jeff watched him stand up straight and, still looking toward the bullpen—toward him, Jeff felt it—hold out his arms, his hands palms up, and shrug, as if to ask Jeff, "How's he look?"

Jeff rocked forward slightly, his entire weight rolling up on the balls of his feet, and spit. He nodded his head twice, exaggerating the movement, telling Daubach what he wanted to hear. Daubach flashed him a thumbs-up. Jeff knew the G.M. was smiling.

Even though he'd felt something alive in the air as J.R. warmed up, Jeff couldn't have imagined the performance the Anointed One turned in that day. J.R. Gold threw a game for the ages. It wasn't perfect—he walked three hitters and gave up four hits—but he rang up twenty-two strikeouts, a major league record. And when J.R. was in the zone as he toed the rubber against the nearly helpless Cardinals' hitters, Jeff was in that zone with him. It felt like a twilight zone. As Jeff sat in the dugout, not only did he sense the crowd noises and ballpark smells as if they came to him filtered through cheesecloth, but he also thought and moved along with J.R. on the mound. When Jeff thought, work him in and set him up for the outside pitch, J.R. would back the hitter away from the plate, then dispose of him with a breaking ball so tantalizingly close to the outside corner that the batter couldn't lay off, swinging over the tops of pitches that dropped as though they'd been rolled off the table. When Jeff thought, no, shake him off—make Martinez give you your pitch, J.R. would shake off Martinez's signal, sending him back through the cycle of signs until he called the pitch J.R. felt would work at that moment against that hitter. Just sitting in the dugout, Jeff began to sweat. When Jeff's arm began to tire slightly in the top of the seventh, he breathed deeply, took a moment to compose himself, and watched J.R. on the mound do the same thing before striking out the hitter. In the eighth, Jeff's legs felt heavy and a slow burn crept through his left thigh. He stood in the dugout, lifted his left foot, and reached back. The stretch ended the burn. Jeff shook each leg, sat down, and watched J.R. make short work of the inning's final hitter.

And in the ninth inning, Cream City clinging to a 1-0 lead, Jeff felt his heart jump into his throat and pound like a sledgehammer. J.R., after recording strikeouts twenty and twenty-one (tying the record), walked the next batter, gave up a single, and issued another walk to load the bases. What the hell is up with that? Jeff thought. Come on, focus—only thing matters here is the batter. That's all. He's yours. Nothing else. Evaluate: stands back in the box, wants a good long look. J.R. removed his cap and wiped his brow with the sleeve of his t-shirt. Jeff ran his hand over the damp spot on his sleeve. He doesn't get it—bat's too slow for the heat. Four-seamer. Watch it explode on him. J.R. threw a fastball past him that he couldn't have touched if he'd started his swing half-way through the last hitter's ups. Yeah, that's right, buddy—couldn't make it happen the first time, I'm betting you won't this time either. J.R. threw him another four-seamer that rose as it reached the plate. Based on the sound of the pitch, the umpire—he couldn't see it any more than the hitter could—called strike two. Jeff knelt on the top step of the dugout. Get it done now—not worth wasting one. Don't let him guess lucky. Pull the string. Ring it up. And though Jeff was aware of himself kneeling, leaning toward the field, watching, he felt as though he were rocking into his motion as J.R. wound up for the final pitch—felt himself stride, felt his pitching arm reach back and sling forward, felt the whisper of horsehide as it left his fingertips, felt the momentum of his body in the follow-through of the delivery, felt the rush that came when the batter swung at air and the umpire theatrically called the third strike.

Jeff beat everyone else to the mound. He threw himself at J.R., who stood tall, arms extended toward the sky, and without meaning to, Jeff knocked him to the ground, his arms encircling him, his cheek pressed against J.R.'s damp neck. A split second later, the rest of the team buried them, and for a time they were a mass of back-slapping, war-whooping joy that spilled onto the grass between home and the hill. The players eventually untangled themselves and managed to lift J.R. to their shoulders, allowing him to bask in the sound of the crowd, a roar that seemed far too raucous for this understandably small, late-season gathering.

Jeff had allowed himself to drift away from the center of the storm and stood on the fringes of the group. He was spent, his body exhausted—as though he'd just spent four hours stacking second crop hay in the mow on a humid July evening—his mind sluggish, slow to acknowledge what had just happened. In a rush, the gauze that had seemed to wrap him all afternoon fell away. Jeff allowed himself to be swept away by it all. He noticed the sound of the exploding fireworks being shot from the top of the scoreboard in left field; the damp smell of the grass in the shadows that slowly crawled across the field; the sight of family and friends alongside the home dugout—Carolyn, seeming to glow even in the shadows, his father and the rest of the contingent cheering with the same pure sense of joy and release as the rest of the crowd; the press of his teammates' bodies as they began a circuit of the field with a beaming J.R. Gold on their shoulders; and the elusive taste forming in the back of his throat, simultaneously horse radish bitter and apple pie sweet.

Jeff told himself, finally, that he knew.

Eighth Inning

In the weeks following J.R.'s emphatic exclamation point on the season, Jeff settled into the rhythms of life on the farm. Early rising had never been a problem for him. Leaning against the warm bodies of the cows as he slipped the black rubber inflations over their teats actually felt good by comparison to the crisp October air he'd walked through to get to the barn. Corn picking progressed methodically—that summer's weather had provided a perfect combination of rain and sun, producing a bumper crop that would fill the cribs to bursting and, Big Al said, let them make a sizeable sale to the grain elevator in town. On days too wet for picking, Jeff worked with his father in the cluttered workshop in the machine shed, assembling assorted boards and sheets of plywood to form a new deer stand that would replace his father's old stand, the one that had blown down, along with the cedar that held it, in an unusually windy stretch in September. They went to meetings with a lawyer to set the language of a land contract, meetings with a banker to make the necessary financial arrangements. On Monday, October 28, the land would change hands. It was land that Otto Luckow had first homesteaded in 1898 and had passed along to his son (Jeff's grandfather), land that had been passed along to Jeff's father when he decided, after returning from a tour in Vietnam in 1968 and two years of piecework at the Kohler plant near Sheboygan, that he was meant to work the soil. The land would become the property of Jeff Luckow.

Jeff spent his evenings with Carolyn. She lived in the house where she'd been raised—hers now that her parents had passed away. She kept the house as Jeff remembered it. The same worn kitchen table, the same green living room carpet, the same varnished black floorboards and wide moldings around the doors and windows. Their conver-sations were exceedingly polite, almost tentative as they tried to reach across the space of the years. The feared that bringing up certain topics or saying the wrong thing might send one—or both—of them scurrying for the safety afforded by saying it was late, that they needed to get up early in the morning. It had been one thing to write letters; it was quite another for them to actually sit next to each other on the same couch in the same living room where they'd once sat late at night, hoping Carolyn's parents wouldn't hear them. So they stuck to safe subject matter—anecdotes from Jeff's years in the sticks, Carolyn teaching at the same school where they'd graduated, what Jeff might do with the farm once it was his.

But after having felt each other out, after gaining their bearings and growing accustomed to the new rhythms of being together, they did, finally, talk about those months following graduation. At times, Jeff felt something begin to open up within him, something that felt fresh and dangerously like a wound. But he managed to push it back and was left with a feeling of great distance—as though a chasm had opened up and stretched between them, even after they'd again learned to hold each other and had finally allowed themselves to express whatever grief remained in them after thirteen years. The tears were, for both of them, brief but real. Jeff felt as if he cried for something inexpressible, something just beyond a wall in his brain that wouldn't allow him to see exactly what was there. He could only hear it, faintly echoing in a place he couldn't rightly call his past or his future, a place Jeff knew he would have to visit sooner or later.

That visit came Sunday, October 27.

The old yellow phone hanging next to the front door of the farmhouse rang twice before Jeff answered. It was Ray Daubach. "Hey, kid," he said, "how'd you like to become the youngest pitching coach in the National League?"

Jeff sat down in the old rocking chair to one side of the door. He didn't know what to say, how to respond—all that came out his mouth was a low "umm…"

"I know, I know," Ray said. "You thought I'd forgotten about you."

Jeff pushed aside the lace curtain his mother had sewn and looked out the window. Big Al was leaning against the light pole and shooting his .30-06, sighting it in for deer hunting. "No…I know the politics on your end of things." Ray had taken his job just prior to the start of Spring Training and had decided to keep the current coaching staff in place for the season rather than dredging the bottom of the managerial pool, the ones who hadn't been hired in the weeks following the World Series.

"I always had you pegged as someone who understood things," Ray said. "One of the reasons you're the best man for the job. Bowie said the same thing when I suggested you."

Jeff didn't answer. He kept watching his father outside. Big Al had set down his gun and started walking toward the target to check his shot placement—confirm what he'd seen through his scope. His limp had grown more pronounced since Jeff had seen him in Arizona that spring. Jeff was glad they'd been able to rig stairs to his deer stand rather than a ladder—he didn't think his father would've been able to make it up if they hadn't, but with his dad, one never knew.

"Hello?" Ray asked. "Earth to Jeff here—one of those farm cats got your tongue? Or maybe one of those lousy rural phone hookups cut us off there for a moment? Things aren't like that in the Show, you know."

Jeff felt his mouth go dry. His tongue felt especially thick when he spoke. "No, I'm here. I just…"

"No need to explain—jumping for joy on the inside," Daubach said. "Too much for words, is that it? Or is this your version of negotiation—want me to show my hand, shoot you some numbers before you give the affirmative? It's a standard contract, the market rate for a pitching coach—trust me, it's way more than you ever made on a minor league contract. And it puts you in the Show."

Jeff exhaled and traced his index finger across the condensation on the window. "I'm sure it's all good, Ray, it's just that—"

"Don't say another word, kid—we'll do this the right way. Let you look things over before you put your name on the line. Have any access to a fax machine up in the sticks?" Ray asked.

"The grocery store here—Owen's Fine Foods," Jeff said.

"...Fine Foods. Got it," Ray said. "I'll fax you a copy of the contract tomorrow morning. Take a day or two, look it over—talk about it with whoever you need to consult when making 'important life decisions' and get back to me with that yes."

Jeff closed his eyes and rested his forehead against his thumb and index finger. He heard the report of Big Al's rifle from outside, muffled by distance and the windowpane, just before Ray delivered his closing line—"And welcome to the Show, kid." Jeff swallowed hard when he heard the click on the other end of the line.

When Jeff arrived at Carolyn's that night, he found that she'd pushed her coffee table to the edge of the living room and had spread a blanket out in front of the television, which was tuned to Game Seven of the World Series, San Francisco at Anaheim. She'd arranged an assortment of ballpark fare on the blanket—foil-wrapped hotdogs, plastic trays of nachos with swimming in orange cheese sauce, an ice-filled bucket packed with soda, light beer, and a bottle of champagne. "I don't think we'd be out of line celebrating what's happening tomorrow," she said when Jeff asked about the seemingly out of place bottle. "It's not every day someone takes over the family farm."

Jeff forced himself to smile. He even chuckled a bit, but he groaned on the inside at Carolyn's reference to his meeting at the bank the next morning, and he felt his cheeks go cold as he sat down next to her on the blanket. Carolyn seemed to glow that evening in the same way she had at Cream City's ballpark almost a month earlier. And like that day, Jeff couldn't decide if his eyes were playing tricks on him—the result of the lighting—or if he saw something no one else could. Also like that day at the ballpark, Carolyn wore the bracelet of freshwater pearls, a fact Jeff noticed when she spooned relish on a hot dog and handed it to him.

They ate quietly as the muted television broadcast the opening innings of the game. Inside, though, Jeff was anything but comfortable. In his head, he heard Ray Daubach's voice over the telephone, and in his mind's eye, he saw his father limping toward the target. As Carolyn talked about her students' responses to Ralph Waldo Emerson's *Self-Reliance*, Jeff mentally broke down the mechanics of J.R. Gold's delivery and imagined ways of putting that poetry into understandable terms that other pitchers could comprehend. As the silent screen broadcast replays of San Francisco's pitcher throwing a hanging breaking pitch that

136

Anaheim's hitter lined to right field to clear the bases, Jeff pictured the brimming corn cribs behind the barn.

And as Carolyn opened the champagne, a sea of bubbles spilling over the green glass bottle, Jeff felt as though he were watching the scene from somewhere outside himself. He watched as she filled two glasses and handed one to him, watched as she raised her glass to her lips and smile at him over the rim, her green eyes alive, the flush of her cheeks obscuring the soft sea of freckles in the already low light of the room. He watched the way her bracelet of freshwater pearls slid away from her wrist as she drank, the way the pearls caught the blue glow of the television screen and radiated a faint aura that reminded Jeff of Christmas lights encased in snow.

Jeff also watched himself drink, but he didn't feel the cool curve of the glass in his hand, didn't feel the bubbling liquid passing between his lips and over his tongue, didn't feel the pleasant burn traveling down his throat and spreading through his body. He continued to be a spectator as Carolyn took his glass and set it alongside hers on an end table before kneeling next to him, leaning in, and very gently kissing him. The kiss went on for a long time, but Jeff remained outside himself. Floating, he watched the way she held him and he held her; the way she eventually ended the kiss, pulled away from him, vaguely smiling, her eyelids heavy, her lips full and red, and began to undress, first herself and then Jeff. And he continued to watch as their bodies reacted to each other's touch, each other's motion, reaching through space and time to find a rhythm they'd once known but had forgotten. At some point, Jeff felt that rhythm building. He tried to pull himself into the scene. He tried to touch her in a way that communicated something very real, but when he felt that rhythm reach a point where neither of them could hold back any longer, he felt himself slipping away again and the sensations that came to him were dull, muted. He lay spent beneath Carolyn, in another place where nothing could reach him—not the gravity of his own exhaustion, not her weight pressing him down into the blanket, into the green carpet that spread around them like outfield grass in an empty ballpark beneath a harvest moon.

When Jeff awoke, he found Carolyn curled tightly against him. The blanket had been pulled up around them, and the television screen was a silent white sea of static, flickering over the room. The clock on the VCR read 1:30, the colon between the one and the three blinking

137

rhythmically. Jeff's head felt as if someone had driven an axe into his forehead, and he winced when he tried to move. Slowly, carefully, he left the blanket, found his clothes draped over the couch, and got dressed.

He walked to the kitchen and drank a glass of water. It was like a shock to his system, and he felt something electrical slither through his body. Fighting back a shiver that made goose bumps stand out from every inch of him, he found a notepad. Across the top was a quote—from a poem, he presumed—*"Do not go gentle into that good night."* He shook his head. He'd never fully understood English teachers—doubted he ever would—and left a two-word note for Carolyn above his signature. He went back to the living room, pulled the blanket tight around Carolyn's bare shoulders, turned off the television, and left the house. He pulled the door closed behind him with a faint click that sounded louder than it really was at that time of the night.

Jeff walked to his car parked at the end of the driveway and climbed in. When he turned the key in the ignition, it came to life—the green glow of the gauges, the faint hiss of the fan, the low sound of the motor. And the music from the speakers, from the tape he rarely removed from the deck—Lyle Lovett and Randy Newmann in their unlikely duet of "Long, Tall Texan." Jeff turned up the volume as he backed out of the driveway and pointed the car toward town.

Main Street was deserted, the windows black in all the storefronts, throwing the reflection of Jeff's headlights back at him as he drove. He turned left where Main intersected with McKenzie in front of St. John's Lutheran and drove past the tall Victorian homes that once must have been elegant and stately, but now only seemed to sag under an invisible weight, badly needing paint, windows, and energy. Jeff pulled into the parking lot of the high school, cut the engine, and simply sat there for several minutes. The bleachers by the football field were a single, hulking shadow. Jeff walked toward the baseball diamond.

He went to the spot where the first base bag would normally be anchored and looked up. The moon was full, he knew, but it failed to break through—only silvering the edges of the clouds slowly creeping across the sky. Jeff liked that, liked the darkness—the way it seemed to stay close to him suited his mood. It helped him think clearly, made him forget about the headache that had greeted him when he woke up in Carolyn's living room.

He began to walk the bases, becoming intensely aware of his body and his surroundings—the uneven feeling of the neglected infield dirt beneath his feet, the stark contrast between the nighttime air that had already left a white coating of frost on the grass and the heat building within him. His legs felt strong, and as he approached second base, he began to jog. Rounding the corner toward third, he felt the natural rhythms of his arms pumping, building momentum, urging his legs to transition from jog to run. As Jeff planted his foot on the spot where third base would have been, he made the wide turn toward home, and his running became an all-out sprint. His shoes, even without the benefit of spikes, broke through the thin crust the frost had created, and they churned the dirt, sending a spray of earth into the air. And just before he reached the plate, Jeff went into a perfect hook slide. He hadn't needed to execute it often as a pitcher, but the skill had stayed with him from his high school days when he played the outfield on days he didn't pitch. Jeff felt the denim of his jeans tearing, the soles of his shoes plowing into the soil and deftly catching the corner of what would have been home plate. For a moment, all sounds ended, replaced by silence as Jeff pushed himself up from the ground. The first sound he heard was the sound of himself inhaling—a deep, stomach-expanding breath of freezing October air that burned his lungs—followed by his coughing as he exhaled. His short puffs of breath formed clouds that blossomed white against the dark sky, and Jeff watched them dissipate, fading to black.

He bent over and swept his hands over torn denim, brushing away the damp soil that clung to him, then took several steps toward the pitchers mound. He stopped halfway between home and the mound and turned around. Linwood's smokestacks were still spitting clouds of smoke into the air. Beyond the black tree line on the northern horizon, the red light of the radio transmission tower on Suring Hill blinked its intermittent warning. Beneath that hill, he knew, his father lay in bed, sleeping for a few more hours before rising to face the chores he would tough out before going to the bank.

Jeff slowly let his eyes focus on things much closer to him. On the hill behind home plate, the elementary school looked down, forming an irregular silhouette against the rows of red pines that stretched away from the building. Atop the low rise halfway between third and first bases, the pitchers rubber was a faint silver slab that glowed for a moment when the moon broke through the clouds. He closed his eyes and breathed deeply; the air had stopped stinging his lungs, and he held it for a long time, feeling the pleasant expansion of his ribs and stomach. He pictured, for a moment as brief as the moon breaking through the clouds,

J.R. Gold…Mario …the Anointed One—pictured what it must be like for a batter to stand in the box and see the man-child launch himself toward the plate. Jeff exhaled and opened his eyes, knowing he'd come home.

Bottom of the Ninth

"You never answered my question, Mr. L—is that what you really want?"

As Annie's question hung in the air, the fax machine came to life, a series of electronic beeps and hisses. The first of several sheets of paper began its slow crawl into the paper tray. Jeff felt his heart jump into his throat, and he looked at the Sun Drop clock. Big Al was expecting him at the bank in five minutes. "That's a tough call, Annie— way tough."

Jeff hadn't bothered going to sleep after his late night visit to the baseball diamond. After he drove home, he went to the upstairs room where his mother had packed away boxes holding the things that had been so important to him in his youth. He pulled the chain that turned on a bare light bulb, and searched until he found the box he wanted. Sitting cross-legged on the bare wood floor, he blew the thin layer of dust from the closed flaps of the box and opened it. First, he pulled out a small plastic container that held the senior pictures of old friends. He spent several minutes shuffling through them until he came to Carolyn's pictures—four poses from Zander Photography in Shawano. She'd worn her hair softly feathered back in the style that had been popular in the late Eighties. In one, she leaned against a doorframe, arms crossed, her smile almost private—like she knew some secret to which anyone looking at the picture would never be privy. Two of the pictures were variations on the classic head shot—angled slightly, looking into the distance somewhere beyond and to one side of the camera. In the final picture, she sat in front of a white backdrop, several large geometric blocks arranged behind her, and she looked back directly from the picture, smiling the purest, sweetest smile Jeff had ever seen. He smiled back at the miniature Carolyn and set the photos on the floor next to him.

He reached back into the box and found the shoebox from an old pair of Converse All-Stars. Opening it, he found neatly banded stacks of baseball cards. He held one of the stacks close to his nose and breathed in the scent of old cardboard. If he focused, he could imagine the stale scent of hard, pink bubble gum. He remembered how, as a boy, he would go into Gillett grocery shopping with his mother and pass over a pair of quarters at the counter of the Ben Franklin in exchange for two packages of Topps baseball cards, tightly wrapped in waxy paper. He looked at the faded shots splashed across the cardboard. The batters posed, glaring

141

back at the camera. The pitchers extended their arms toward the foreground, following through on imaginary pitches. He scanned the rows and columns of tiny numbers arranged on the dull backs of the cards. He used to spend hours with them—creating dream teams, committing their statistics to memory. He played out imaginary games on the floor of his bedroom, wondering what it must feel like to leave home, to make your way to the major leagues, to find your picture printed on a bubble gum card. Jeff wondered what J.R. Gold would look like on his rookie card.

Jeff reached into the box one last time, pulling out an old baseball glove—his first mitt, given to him by Big Al for his seventh birthday. He'd used it through t-ball and Little League. Jeff slipped it onto his right hand. It was too small for him now, and the heel of his hand stuck out from the opening at the bottom of the mitt, but he kept it on anyway. With his balled left fist, he punched the creased pocket, his skin making a faint slapping sound on the leather. For several weeks after that birthday, he'd slept with the glove, cradling it in the crook of his arm and holding it tight against him as he listened to soft rustle of leaves from the box elder outside his window, whispering him to sleep. For a long time, Jeff sat there on the floor. He looked at the pictures of Carolyn. He flipped through stacks of baseball cards. He ran his fingers over the dry, cracked leather of the glove, promising himself that he'd rub life back into it using soft cheesecloth and neat's foot oil. All the while, Jeff tried to triangulate his future somewhere amid the remnants of his past.

He finally heard the alarms go off in Big Al and Jody's rooms. Jeff straightened his stiff legs, stood up, and went to his room, where he pulled on his work clothes, then went outside to begin preparations for milking. Jeff talked little during the morning chores—he didn't need to, as Big Al talked enough for both of them. At one point during the chores, Jeff almost told his father about the fax that would be coming that morning, about what it would mean, but he simply couldn't bring himself to do it. And after chores, after he'd showered and slipped into the uncomfortable suit he hated to wear, Jeff nearly picked up the phone and dialed the high school, to see if Carolyn was available, but he decided to let the handset rest in its cradle.

When Big Al had come into the kitchen, wearing a tie wide enough to be a bib and a smile wide enough to drive a small tractor through, Jeff said that they should take separate cars into town, that he wanted to get his oil changed at Zahn's Garage and maybe stop at the grocery store. Big Al had liked the idea—"Maybe pick up a couple of t-bones for the grill, hmmm?" he said. "We'll certainly have some things to celebrate today." He'd patted Jeff's shoulder and limped out to the garage.

Now Annie placed her hands on the counter and spoke. "Am I to assume this transmission has something to do with your decision, Mr. L?"

Jeff watched the last sheet of the fax drop into the tray. "Who's the nosey one now?"

"Turnabout's fair play," Annie said. "And in case you forgot, in a small town, everyone minds everyone else's business, for better or worse." She smiled at Jeff—he couldn't be sure exactly what it meant—and turned to the machine. She picked up the sheets and handed them to him.

"Thanks," he said. Jeff felt weak, and the sheets of paper trembled in his hands. "Is there somewhere I can be alone for a minute?"

Annie led him to a small office in the rear of the store. She left him there. Jeff didn't bother closing the door—he just sat down at the battered desk and began to look over the contents of the fax.

The contract wasn't unlike those he'd signed as a player—the same legalese, the same clauses and conditions, the same sections and sub-sections. It was exactly what Ray had promised. Jeff knew that in relative terms, the salary wasn't huge, but it dwarfed any figure he'd ever seen as a minor league player. And he knew that putting his name on the line meant that he'd made it—not in the way he'd embraced in his dreams since childhood, but he'd made it. He thought of J.R., and especially of that final game. He hated to admit it, but in a way Jeff couldn't even begin to express, that day had been more gratifying than any outing he'd ever had on the mound himself. He thought of his father sitting at the bank and broke into a cold sweat as he pictured him shooting the breeze with the loan officer. He thought of Carolyn—God, Carolyn—standing in front of thirty high school juniors, doing her level best to help them unlock the mysteries she loved. He wondered how she had responded to the simple note he'd left on her kitchen counter. And he thought of Ray Daubach in his office in Cream City—helluva lot nicer than this, for sure, he thought—waiting for his response.

Jeff sat at the desk, staring for what felt like forever at the blank line awaiting his signature, bouncing his leg under the desktop. He checked his shirt pocket for the pen he'd tucked there before leaving home, pulled it out, and tested it on a notepad before tucking it back into his pocket. Breathing deeply, forcing himself to push back the nervous shakes that made him feel limp as a rubber band, Jeff carefully folded the faxed contract and tucked it into the inner pocket of his suit coat. He stood up, walked through the office door, and down the aisle past the freezer case, toward where Annie had resumed her work behind the low Plexiglas window. He didn't look at her as he walked past, moving toward the labored hiss of the automatic doors leading to the parking lot. "Off to chase dreams, Mr. L?" she called after him.

Jeff didn't stop to answer her. He heard the doors groan shut behind him and walked to his car. As he keyed open the driver's side lock, he looked west down Main Street—toward the bank, and beyond that, the high school. He got into the car, started it, and pulled into the street, crossing the path of a souped-up 4 x 4 rumbling past, heading west. He turned up the volume on his radio as he drove east, away from the farm, toward the intersection of Main and Highway 32, which he would take until he hit the interstate, going south, sliding into the passing lane and stepping the accelerator to the floor. At the stop sign before pulling onto the highway, he pictured his father in the banker's office and thought of the dollar figure on the contract in his suit. He wondered what a graduate of the dairy program at the UW would command in salary as a herd manager. He thought of Carolyn reciting lines of poetry. He thought of his note to her, and realized that whether it was adequate didn't really matter. His arms still felt limp as he turned the steering wheel, guiding his car onto the highway, but his hands clutched the steering wheel tightly, his knuckles turning white as he finally whispered his answer to Annie's parting question. "They're the only things worth chasing."

ABOUT THE AUTHOR

Scott Winkler grew up on a small family dairy farm in Gillett, Wisconsin, where—aside from the lessons instilled by his family and farm life—he was nurtured by books and the radio broadcasts of Bob Uecker. After graduating from St. Norbert College, he began his teaching career in the Green Bay Area Public Schools, caught the writing bug, and did his graduate studies at the University of Wisconsin-Milwaukee. His fiction, poetry, and academic writing have appeared in numerous journals. Scott currently lives in Northeast Wisconsin with his daughter and teaches at Green Bay West High School.

www.ingramcontent.com/pod-product-compliance
Lightning Source LLC
Chambersburg PA
CBHW070044260626
47159CB00005B/2120